"Why do you not see.

Jordh asked. "Once you knew the ring for what it is, and yet you have forgotten. Do you believe that you can use the ring for good?"

"I know that I can," Odhinn said. "I would trick it into doing good, only twice or three times to give the power I need to defeat my enemies. Then, I promise you, I would throw it into the sun."

"No," Jordh replied, "the ring would possess your mind and will. You would use it freely and consider yourself justified. Yes, you would consider yourself overlord of the nine realms . . ."

REVENGE OF THE VALKYRIE

Thorarinn Gunnarsson

ACE BOOKS, NEW YORK

REVENGE OF THE VALKYRIE

An Ace Book/published by arrangement with
the author

PRINTING HISTORY
Ace edition/August 1989

ISBN: 0-441-72359-4

Ace Books are published by The Berkley Publishing Group,
200 Madison Avenue, New York, New York 10016.
The name ''ACE'' and the ''A''
logo are trademarks belonging to
Charter Communications, Inc.
PRINTED IN THE UNITED STATES OF AMERICA

10 9 8 7 6 5 4 3 2 1

PROLOGUE

Here continues the tale of the Rhinegold, and the great Ring of Power that was made thereof. Great indeed were the powers of the ring, great enough to make a mortal into a god and to give powers to an immortal beyond all reckoning. But the tale that is woven about it is a long and bitter one, for it left only suffering and sorrow whenever it touched the lives of gods and men.

Andvari the dwarf first possessed the Rhinegold, and he bore it many years and never suspected its true worth. And it is his curse that the Rhinegold carries, that it should always betray the hand that bears it. So he pronounced when the gold was stolen from him by Loki of the Flames. Then the mortal Hreidmar had it of Loki, and it was he who made it into a ring by the power of lightning . . . and it was he who was first destroyed by its terrible curse at the hands of his own sons. Then Reginn and Fafnir took the ring and fled into the far north to escape justice for their evil deed, thinking to use its great powers to found a grand kingdom for themselves. And there they died by each other's hand.

And yet the tale of the Rhinegold and the Ring of Power was not yet at an end but indeed had just begun. For Jordh, the living spirit of the world of Midhgardh, knew the gold for the evil thing it was, and she sought above all else its final destruction. Thus, by her command, the spirit of Fafnir was restored to life in the form of a mighty icedrake, and he took the ring into his cold lair to guard it well through the years, caring not for its promises of power but commanded to keep it hidden until the day of its final destruction.

But Jordh remained uneasy, and she bespoke the Nornir, as Mimir, the spirit of the great World-tree Yggdrasill, had taught her. The Nornir were the living spirits of future history, each one a possible path that the days and years ahead might take, although only one would come to be. And they showed her a vision of a terrible future, and it alarmed her as nothing ever had before. For almost every Norn, every strand of destiny, spoke to her of terrible destruction, whatever she did to divert it.

But she also knew that she must try, for the evil that she saw in many of the possible futures was lessened by her intercession. And in some there was a brighter future lying beyond many dark and terrible days. Then Jordh took long and careful council with Mimir, and through Mimir with her sisters, the spirits of the eight worlds above and below her. And they chose the future that they thought best, one in which the destruction of the days ahead would give way to a better time beyond, in which so many of the evils of the nine worlds would be destroyed and forgotten, and the good would survive and prosper. And so they began the long and careful work of making their one dream of a better future into a reality.

For now the problem of how to begin remained, but it was one that Jordh could do something about. She spoke to Mimir a final time, and he told her what she needed to know.

CHAPTER ONE

Winter lay harsh and heavy over the northlands of the nine worlds, the later part of winter that was bitterly cold and dry just before the coming of the first hint of spring. Deadly winds raked the barren mountains of the Nidhavellir and swept across the empty plains and plateaus of Jotunheim. A heavy burden of snow bent the evergreen branches of the forests of the elfworld, and even the great rivers, swift Tungljos and deep Glaervatna, were in danger of freezing. Midhgardh also knew a winter that was deep, brooding and dangerous, as if all life held its breath in fearful anticipation of the brighter days of a spring that would never come. The younger days of the nine realms were past and forgotten, when great beasts had dwelled in vast, steamy forests and winter was not much unlike summer. Winters were long and cold now, hinting that the Great Winter was coming again.

Only on the great plateau of Asgardh, the citadel of the Aesir, did the hand of winter lay lightly, for those who dwelled there would have it so. High though it was, the winds that swept the plateau were cold but never harsh, and the snow and sleet always passed to either side. The trees and exotic plants of their gardens did not wither and shed their leaves but only ceased to grow for a time, sleeping through the cold winter until the warm, gentle breezes of spring stirred them again to life. Squirrels harvested nuts that did not fall through the winter, and some of those squirrels that haunted the gardens of Idhunn had seen the passing of many thousands of winters.

Winter was a gentle time in Asgardh, a time of quiet and of sleep. But this winter was quieter than most, although it was a restless stillness as if of nervous waiting. Odhinn sat alone in his great hall and brooded on matters the nature of which no one else could guess. Loki was conspicuously absent, so it was known that he had been at the heart of whatever trouble had befallen. Thor, who alone knew what had happened in the wilderness of Midhgardh, remained stubbornly silent. The Valkyries annoyed Brynhild for whatever news she might have, but she claimed to know no more than her sisters. And that was the truth, although she would not have spoken anyway. Thus the stillness in the air was that of mystery and somber brooding and an unwillingness to break the fragile peace. The inhabitants of Asgardh knew only that something had gone very wrong, and they were afraid.

It was on the morning of such a day that danger came. The horn of Heimdall echoed throughout the complex of Asgardh suddenly and without warning, signalling a breach of the great world-gate. Odhinn, sitting alone in Valhalla, leaped up and stood facing in that direction, spear in hand, as the watch-wolves Geri and Freki sprang up and rushed to stand guard over him, one to either side.

"Mind your furry friends," a female voice spoke unseen out of the air, echoing through the empty hall. "They may not harm me, nor have I any wish to harm them in turn."

"Who are you?" Odhinn demanded, trying to identify the curious presence that he felt.

"Need you ask?" the voice replied. "You know me

well, although we do not speak often. Still, it has not been long since we last exchanged words, and I doubt that you have forgotten. Although it might well be that you prefer to forget."

"Will you not speak plainer than that?" Odhinn asked impatiently. "You sound as though you are speaking to yourself. Who are you?"

"Perhaps it is that you simply did not expect to find me here."

"Jordh, is that truly you?" he asked hesitantly. "Indeed I did not expect to find you here. You cannot be here."

"I am not here," Jordh replied. "And yet I am. But enough. Go to the Garden of Idhunn, and I will meet you there."

"But, Jordh. . . ."

"No, save your questions until then," she said quickly. "I probably will not answer anyway. Be quick!"

"Jordh!" Odhinn called impatiently, but he knew that she was gone. He stood for a moment, wondering if he really wanted to hear what she had come to tell him, then snatched up his spear and hurried off as the wolves watched in bewilderment.

Idhunn's garden was not far, but Odhinn begrudged the minutes that it took him to walk, and those who saw him striding intently through the avenues of Asgardh did not dare to call to him. Whatever Jordh had come to say, he could well guess that it was not to his best interest; Jordh would not trouble herself for his sake. Still, he had to know the news she bore, for good or ill, and above all he wanted to know how she had passed the world-gate. That, by all he knew, was impossible. One of the reasons that the Aesir had retreated into Asgardh was the belief that she could not trouble them there.

He found the Garden of Idhunn vacant, and for that he was glad. He did not want the words of Jordh to be known until he had time to weigh them. He began to search cautiously up and down the narrow paths, checking all the places in that lush garden where Jordh might be hiding. There were indeed few places where she might be without danger of the heat of her form setting fire to the thick growth of exotic plants.

"Jordh!" he called at last, despairing of his search.

"If you are searching for me, then that is a pointless task," she replied suddenly. "I am here, but not in the form that you have always known me."

He turned to follow that voice but saw nothing. He could barely sense her presence, although he knew that she was slowly circling around him.

"Do you think that I have only one form?" she asked. "I can be what I wish. The form that I have always shown you was to remind you of the power I possess. But I can also be as subtle as the breeze."

And to prove it, she vanished from his senses completely. Odhinn planted his spear firmly and smiled.

"So you say," he responded. "But perhaps this is all the power that you can bring out of your realm. You said yourself that you are not really here. Perhaps this is only a shadow of yourself."

"A shadow?" she asked. Suddenly she blazed forth like a small sun hovering above the stony path, shining with such fierce radiance that Odhinn was forced to turn away. "Do you call this a shadow?"

"Enough!" Odhinn cried, and the light vanished. "But how have you accomplished this? You are part of the fabric of your own realm and cannot leave it."

"Do you seek the answer in the hope that you can guard against future intrusions?" Jordh inquired. "You cannot. But I will tell you this much. I have phased through the fabric of space, creating my own gate, or at least a window that I can peek through and reach through at need, carrying it with me as I go. I first used your own world-gate as a point of reference, but now I can phase through as I wish.''

"Which sounds like a great deal of trouble," Odhinn remarked. "I hope that the news you bear is important and not just more of your vague warnings."

"My warnings are not vague; you choose to disregard them," she said as she approached him slowly. "But you may judge that for yourself. Come. Let us walk together while we speak."

"I never thought you to be on anyone's side but your own," Odhinn said, walking slowly along the wooded path with her unseen presence at his side. "Why are you now so supportive of my cause?"

"I am not. You are important to my cause. I have seen a part of the future, Lord of the Aesir. And I pity you."

This time Odhinn did pause and stare, except that there was nothing to stare at. He continued on, "You have had conversation with the Nornir."

"I have," Jordh replied. "I began to wonder about the ring. I wondered if I would be able to keep it safe and out of the hands of you or anyone else. And, if I did lose it, what great evil would be done with it. You know, I suppose, what became of the ring?"

"A dragon has it," Odhinn said. "That much my Valkyries have been able to determine."

"And you have not tried to take it?"

"I know you better than that!" he said, laughing. "I knew that you would be true to your word and bar me from taking it."

"That is wise," Jordh remarked succinctly. "Perhaps you do not know that this dragon is in fact Fafnir Hreidmarsson? And so you see that you are still bound by the promise that you made and cannot take the ring from him without breaking it."

"So I see," Odhinn said thoughtfully. "Now I am bound to spare a dragon. How did you accomplish that?"

"I associate with some very unusual people. Hel, for one. Also those you call Nidhavellir, Alfheim, Jotunheim and Asgardh. I have eight good friends in all, and Mimir as well."

"And you are all conspiring against me?" Odhinn assumed.

"We have all seen what the future holds," Jordh continued. "We have a common goal, to oppose evil and to help what is good to survive what is to come and see a better time beyond. Whether or not we are against you depends upon you, if you will fight for what you claim to uphold and not just to preserve your own power and authority. And if you will leave the ring alone."

"So it again comes back to the ring with you," Odhinn observed as he turned down a short side path. At its end was a stone bench, surrounded by high hedges on nearly every side. "Why do you fear it so?"

"Why do you not see it for what it is and fear it as well?" Jordh asked in return. "Once you did know, and yet you have forgotten."

"That was a very long time ago," Odhinn said wearily as he sat down on the bench. "I was much younger then, much less experienced. I was like you. I saw things only in terms of black and white, good and evil, yes and no. But these are complex matters that I face. My enemies are subtle and cunning. Evil things can be used for good, and small evils can be done with the knowledge that a greater good will come of those acts."

"You believe that you can use the ring for good?"

"I know that I can," Odhinn said and looked up at where he thought her to be. "Do not misjudge me. I would not use it with impunity, but with cunning and great caution. I would trick it into doing good, only twice or three times to give me the power that I need to defeat my enemies. Then, I promise you, I will have it cast into the heart of the sun.''

''Then you also believe that you are immune to its curse?''

Odhinn laughed. ''Surely, my old friend, you do not believe in curses!''

''I know that the ring would possess the mind and will of its bearer,'' Jordh answered. ''And I do not believe that you can resist its lure. Soon you would use it as freely as you desire and consider yourself justified. Yes, you would consider yourself overlord of the nine realms, and all things would either bend to your rule or be destroyed. Already you are forgetting your purpose, that it is the good that you are supposed to nurture and protect, not your own authority.''

''If not for my authority, the three races would be at the mercy of all evil things!''

''But for your interference, there never would have been the world-gates to allow evil things to invade other realms,'' Jordh responded quickly and harshly. ''The nine realms belong to themselves. I am the one authority within Midhgardh, not you. I see you as little different from your enemies.''

''I have the power. . . .''

''You *had* the power, but gave up the greater part of it and now hunger for what you once threw away. You had purpose, and forgot it in your conceit. Tell me why I should not destroy you where you stand and remove such a potential for evil!''

Odhinn leaped up in alarm and held out his spear threateningly, but an invisible force ripped it from his hands and flung it aside. He backed away cautiously, for he no longer knew where Jordh was or trusted what she might do.

"But fear me not," Jordh continued after a long, tense moment. "I see that you have as much potential for good as for evil, and I hope that you will do what is best when you hear of the future that I have seen."

Odhinn quickly retrieved his spear, then stood facing her. "Tell me of it, then. For if you have seen what fills even you with such fear that you would make the effort to come into this realm to tell me of it, then I will listen."

"What do you know of the Nornir?"

"I know of them, that they in some way know the future," Odhinn replied. "I have heard it said that they are three. Some say that they represent the past, the present and the future. Others say that one is the central stream of time leading into the future and the others are the extremes to either side of her, diverting the stream of time first one way and then another in their strife. But the truth of the matter is, I am sure, far more complex than that."

"So it is," Jordh agreed. "You know little of the truth. For now it is enough that you know that they can see all possible futures and can make small predictions of what will be. But they can say nothing with absolute certainty, for new possibilities are always emerging. The stream of time follows the channel cut by the events of the present. We can alter that path by our acts and deeds, but the scale of possibilities is simply too vast for any of us to control."

"What will be, will be," Odhinn observed. "But the Nornir might back some judgment through the overview that they alone may see."

"That is so. Many paths may lead to the same end. And since the forging of the ring, nearly all paths lead into a single future. The Nornir see a time of strife and conflict that will end in destruction such as has not been known since the rising of the world-tree and the fusing of the nine realms. Indeed they see the destruction of all life within the nine realms, all beings both good and evil, all plants and animals, even the Aesir themselves. They see the destruction even of the spirits of the nine worlds, so that no life will ever come again.''

Odhinn sat for a long moment in silence, stroking his beard as he thought furiously of what he might do to avert that destruction, assuming, as always, that it was his responsibility alone. But there were no answers. At last he looked up at Jordh.

''This vision of the future, is there nothing more?'' he asked. ''How will it come about?''

''Why do you want to know?'' Jordh asked. ''It is terrible!''

''I must know, all the same.''

Jordh paused a moment, as if considering what she must do. ''Yes, there is a greater vision of what will come to pass.''

A spark sprang into the air before him, spinning rapidly as it expanded into a sphere of dense white mist. Then the ball of mist ceased to revolve, and its layers pulled back so that Odhinn could look inside and see dim visions of the things and events she described. Often the same event was repeated many times and in each passing was different in small ways. But the end was always the same.

''The events that lead the stream of time through the present and into the future have been long in the shaping,'' Jordh began even before the sphere of seeing opened. ''Here are your chief enemies. Utgardh-Loki, who seeks to rebuild the nine realms into his own kingdom, and which he will likely manage far better than you have done. Here also is Surtur of Muspell. He had the power to stand against you even in your former days. Other enemies you have beyond count; the kings of the burrow-realms of the dark elves and the war-chieftains of the trolls under their Queen of the Ironwood. Dragons of fire and ice and water.

One day they will all come against you, more enemies than you ever thought you had.

"First there will come the death of one you hold dear and the treachery of one you have long held in your trust. There will come a winter that does not end and a night that has no dawn. For seven years will the cold and darkness last, and then the traitor of Asgardh will lead your enemies against you. Mountains will fall, and seas will swell out of their beds. The hound that Hel has long kept chained will be set free, and the wolf you would not slay will break his chain. The great serpent of Midhgardh will rise from the depths.

"Your enemies will gather in Midhgardh at the base of the bridge Bifrost, and they will hold the world-gate open and besiege you at your main gate. Thor shall fight the dragon of Midhgardh, and both shall die. Tyr will slay Garm, the hound of Nifheim, only to die as well. Heimdall and the traitor of Asgardh will battle to the death before the very gate. And you yourself, Odhinn Allfather, will be devoured by the great wolf Fenrir, though he will soon die himself.

"Then Muspell will have his victory and seat himself upon the very throne of Valhalla. Thus he will accomplish his great purpose, the one purpose to his very existance; to destroy all life. He will release his flames and allow them to wash through the world-gates into all the realms like a vast flood. The land will be seared dry and hard and the seas will turn to steam in a single flash. The sky will be blasted away, and all the worlds will be laid barren and lifeless to the icy cold of the starrealm."

The visions faded and the sphere of mist slowed away into the cool morning air. Odhinn sat for a long time, brooding in silence, and it gave Jordh no satisfaction to see that he was pale and shaken. Almost she pitied him, but not quite. He was doomed, and that doom was of his own making.

"And so it will end for us all," he said at last. "Even yourself."

"Even me," Jordh admitted. "Although it did not begin that way, I have become tied to the life about me. As it has developed, so have I. And when it dies, then shall I as well."

"But must it be so?" Odhinn demanded as he looked up at her. "Is there no other future that the Nornir have revealed to you?"

"There were many futures shown to me," she answered. "Most end as I have said. But some ended differently. It is also likely that the flames of Surtur will be weak in comparison. Then the seas and the sky will endure little damage. The lands will be burned barren and dead, but after a long winter the life that I and my sisters have been able to protect will come forth again to begin almost as it was before, save that all evil creatures will be gone forever. That is the future that I wish to see."

"But how is that difference made?" Odhinn asked. "Surtur's powers are his own, unless they are in some way diminished."

"Or supplemented."

He looked up at her in surprise and fear. "You mean to say. . . ."

"In one future Surtur will have the ring, and by its power the destruction will be complete," Jordh explained. "In the other he will not, for it will have been destroyed."

"And how does he come by the ring? Not by my hand, for if I had it, then none of my enemies could defeat me."

"Indeed by your hand shall he have it," Jordh answered. "It will not give you the power to defeat your enemies, but will betray you as it has betrayed every hand that has held it. Fenrir will devour you, and the ring will destroy him with flame from within. Then Freyr will take the ring, and Surtur will slay him on the very steps of Valhalla and have it in turn.

"And do not ask, for I will tell you now. In no future of what will come to pass will you defeat your enemies. With the ring or without it, your destruction is assured if you stay to do battle. You have only a single chance for survival."

"And what do you advise me to do?" Odhinn asked.

"My advice is that you seize your chance and flee the nine worlds," she replied. "Abandon the shapes that you have assumed, and return to the starrealm. And when you go, I ask that you take the ring and cast it into the sun."

"But if we return to what we were, then our full powers would be restored, and we would be able to defeat our enemies."

"That, too, is foreseen," Jordh said. "But you cannot destroy Surtur without releasing his flames. The great destruction is assured either way, but if the Aesir stay to fight then many would be destroyed. At least there will be new life after the flames."

"And if we do depart?"

"Then your enemies will fight among themselves, and Surtur will go against Utgardh-Loki for possession of abandoned Asgardh. He will have his victory, or he will fail, and the end will be the same."

"And if we destroy the world-gates?" Odhinn asked.

"Do you not understand?" Jordh asked impatiently. "One of your servants will betray you. He will show your enemies the secret of opening new world-gates, and still the ending is unchanged."

"And if I can find the traitor. . . ."

"He will escape you, and take dire vengeance," Jordh said and paused. "Odhinn, you cannot win the last battle, nor can you prevent the destruction. Anything that you might hope to do will be in vain, for nothing can be done. Choose well!''

And then she was gone, before Odhinn could say another word. Thus he was left to consider all that she had told him and come to some decision of his own. He did not doubt anything that Jordh had told him. The capacity was not within her to lie. And yet he also did not doubt that she was hiding something from him, the most important part of this riddle of what was to be. For she had said not a word of her own plans, of what she would be doing to shape all the possibilities into a future of her own choosing. He thought he knew what her choice was, and how she would go about it. He knew as well that he was a very large part of her plans, a part that had to be removed before she could ever have her way.

Odhinn knew what he had to do once he was spared a few minutes with his own council. And he realized that this game was ultimately his, for he had nothing to lose. Jordh was very right about one thing. He and his kind could abandon the lives that they had made for themselves and return to the starrealm. But there was no reason why they should do so immediately. He could stay for now, play this game and see if he could win. And when it became obvious that he could not, then he could leave it, take the ring with him so that Surtur could not have a complete victory, and leave the nine realms for life to start again. He could even return in some future age and start again.

And so he sat back in his contemplations and smiled at Jordh's simplicity, very satisfied with himself. Of course she had known that he would guess the missing pieces of her puzzle. Perhaps she had even known herself what his own decision would be and had still found herself compelled to attempt to mislead him. What he failed to consider was that he had just come to the very decision that she had wanted him to make.

CHAPTER TWO

Odhinn sat long on his high seat in lofty Valhalla and in the quiet solitude of the garden of his own palace, Vingolf, and considered carefully how he might set about to recover the ring, having decided that his only hope lay in its possession. He knew from the start that it would not be an easy task and likely a dangerous one if Jordh caught him meddling in this affair. He now had not only his old enemies to contend with, but now Jordh and her sisters as well. Jordh possessed both the greater power and the greater patience, and yet patience and subtlety were his best weapons for achieving his ends.

He knew from the first that he could never take the ring openly by force. Even if all his other councils were awry, he knew that he lacked even a quarter of the power he would need to face Jordh in her own element and that, as she had once said, she never slept, but was well aware of the deeds of either himself or his servants within her own realm. Therefore, any agent he sent to slay Fafnir and take the ring would have to be one who did not openly or knowingly serve his will, in accordance with the terms of the oath that he had sworn to Hreidmar Arnorsson and which Jordh meant to hold him to. And the only way to insure that, it seemed to him, was to be very sure that no one knew his plans but himself.

The next problem lay in finding the proper servant, one who would escape the notice of Jordh and yet be able to retrieve the ring from Fafnir's icy den. None of his own servants were suitable, of course. Any one of the Valkyries, although well able to handle the likes of Fafnir, would be known at once. Any servant of power, no matter what form it took, would be easily recognized to whomever had the ability to see beneath the outer form.

And while Odhinn refused to accept that the curses of a dwarf were to any effect, he did not deny that the ring appeared to carry a curse of its own making. He trusted in his ability to refuse the lure of the ring and maintain mastery over it, but he doubted that many of his servants, and none who could escape Jordh's notice, would be so immune. Loki had fallen into its trap as easily as any mortal. There remained the problem. Jordh would be aware of any who had the power to resist the lure of the ring, while any who were small enough to escape her notice would be easy victims of its curse.

Now when Odhinn considered all of these things together, he soon knew the answer to what he sought. Indeed, considering all that was required, there was only one solution. A mortal man would pass unnoticed where all others would be marked, for Midhgardh was the world of men, and Jordh paid little mind to their comings and goings. A young man of the northlands, a warrior of the tall, fair race that sailed their sleek ships on rivers and fjords, might well have the strength and skill in arms to slay the dragon Fafnir.

But to defeat the dragon, he would need an exceptional warrior, one with strength, quickness and skill well beyond the limits of other men. One who had the abilities of one of the Aesir but who was still a mortal in all other ways, with no great powers that might betray him to Jordh. A warrior of a mortal race descended of himself, into which was bred strength, agility and courage far beyond the measure of other men. A champion to win the ring and then surrender it freely. For Odhinn knew and trusted the hearts of valiant men, and he knew that they would not easily be corrupted even by the terrible power of the ring, not if they were clear of conscience and honest in both their thoughts and deeds.

For Odhinn knew that it would be many long years, perhaps even several lifetimes of men, before Jordh would relax her vigilance and Odhinn would be able to seize his chance. Now he would lay the seeds of his plans and bring forth a race born of his own being, to await the day when the greatest among them would stand ready to serve his needs.

As that same winter was drawing near its end, Odhinn quietly and secretly departed from Asgardh, leaving Thor and Freyr to watch the affairs of the nine realms. He entered Midhgardh stealthily, not by the main gate where the crystal bridge stood, but by one of the hidden lesser gates. He took what measures he could to subdue his powers and to lay a barrier of darkness about him against those who possessed the inner sight. In this way he passed silently and unseen through the wilds of the northlands until he came to the lower reaches of the river Hronn.

The Hronn lay north and somewhat east of the great Rhine, paralleling its course for the most part only two hundred miles away. Between them lay the deep lake Vidvatn, where the elves had built their gray towers on the island of Gronnfjall. The Hronn was a long river but not so great as the Rhine, for the land about it was hilly and poor. Thus few men lived along its length, and it was a sparse, remote region compared to the Rhinelands.

Near its mouth the Hronn passed through a large area of thick forest amid the lowland plains. Dragons had lived there, as had bands of dark elves and trolls cut off from their gates, so the forest had come to be a place of fear. Men would take the river that passed through it, or even enter it at need, but none would dwell there, and those who did enter did not stay long.

But Odhinn came there now, for this forest was to his liking. Myrkdreyma it was called, for men who slept at night beneath its trees were said to relive the days of evil it had seen. Odhinn renamed it Vargarbraut, the Wolf Path, and the deep, dark caves where trolls and dragons had dwelled he cleaned and freshened, and called them Vargarstedhur. These were indeed more fitting names, for in that forest there still lived a number of the Great Wolves that had flourished before the coming of men, twice as large as common wolves and twice as cunning. Only the wolves of Jotunheim were larger still.

When all was ready Odhinn took the form of one of those immense wolves, and he went into the night to call to him females of that land. Nine she-wolves came to his call, and they sat in a circle about him on a hill under the stars. Odhinn sang to them and cast spells upon them that gave them intelligence and wisdom and the power of speech, and he named himself their lord and spoke to them of his plans. Then he mated with them, each on every following night, and he took them to live in the caves that he had prepared.

Odhinn returned to Asgardh soon after, for he had many important matters to attend to elsewhere. But the nine wolves he left in the care of their own kind, for the entire pack had come to him before he had departed. He had cast spells upon them as well, and they had claimed him for their lord. He left them with instructions to care for his nine mates and to guard them against all dangers. Then he left quietly in the night while none were about to see him go, for he did not want them to know who he was.

"I am a servant of the Aesir," he said when they asked him. "For the wolf is revered by them as the most wise and noble of animals. Therefore, they have chosen you, the greatest of all wolves, to bring forth a new race of men, greater than all other men, for they will possess your strength and courage. As for myself, I am the most trusted servant of the Lord of the Aesir, and I do his work for him which he is not free to do himself. For that reason I am called the Wanderer."

The wolves were in fact very pleased with their task. The Wanderer had given them speech and far greater understanding, so that they now comprehended many of the things that they had never before questioned, and they found a new purpose in life that they had never known. Every new thing they learned surprised them, and they marveled that they could have ever walked through life with the ignorance of animals, with few thoughts and fewer ways to share them.

The harshness of that terrible winter soon passed into a warm and bountiful spring, and that in turn to a gentle summer. The wolves of the Vargarbraut Forest prospered, for they found new and quicker ways to catch their game and were never hungry and had more time for play and speech among themselves. The nine mates of the Wanderer felt new life within them near the end of spring, but it came later than they had anticipated and was slower in coming than they had always remembered. The Wanderer had warned them that this would be so, and they were not greatly concerned.

The leader of the pack in the Wanderer's absence was Bren Skoggi, so named because his fur was darker gray than that of most, and he disappeared more quickly into the shadows of the forest. Megelna Gafadhur was his

mate, and she was called that because she was the most
clever and gifted of the wolves; she first compiled their
lore into verse, and at night she sang to the pack songs that
the Wanderer had taught her and later those that she made
herself. But she was also one of the mates of the Wanderer, and she spoke for her sisters and eased their fears
when they were anxious.

When autumn came at last the wolves could scarcely
contain their excitement, for not only would the Wanderer
return to them soon, but his children would be born a short
time after. The frosts came at night, and the leaves turned
red and gold and soon began to fall. Then one night the
Wanderer returned quietly as they sat and listened to the
stories of old Kelan. At first they were startled, then they
leaped up and ran about howling in delight.

"I cannot see why you are surprised, for I have returned
when I promised," the Wanderer told them. "But I have
not come alone. Roskva the elf-maiden has come with me,
and she will teach you and do many things for you. Do not
fear her, even though she looks like a young girl of the
human kind, for she is a wood-elf and much at home in
such a place as this."

He turned and called, and a moment later Roskva stepped
out of the shadows. The wolves were indeed afraid of her
at first. Too fresh in their minds were the memories of
hunters and their hounds and arrows that brought silent
death. She wore the clothes of her own kind, tunic and
pants and light boots of the forest's deep green, and she
was swift and tireless and in all ways familiar and confident in the wild.

The wolves were not long in becoming used to her and
even to appreciate what she could do. She made hearth in
a sheltered place near the front of their caves and laid a
fire, and at night she kept a bright and cheerful blaze for
them to sit about. She sang them songs and told them

stories such as wood-elves knew, and she taught them her lore and to read the writing of her people. Roskva alone of the inhabitants of Asgardh knew something of Odhinn's plans, but he had told her no more than he had found necessary.

Soon after the Wanderer's return, the first of his children was born, the offspring of Megelna Gafadhur. But when Roskva carried the little one out for all the wolves to see, they were surprised, and they wondered if there had been some mistake. They had expected a human child, according with the Allfather's plans. And yet what Roskva brought them first to see was in every way a young cub of their own kind, but seemingly weeks rather than minutes old, and his eyes were open. Only the Wanderer was delighted and smiled at their consternation.

"Do not be alarmed," he told them. "Look upon the wonders of the Aesir! For your children will be neither wolves nor men, but either at will. He and his brothers and sisters will be as one of your own for their first year, and they will grow swifter than human kind, and thereafter be able to change their shapes at will. That, as well as their strength and courage, are their gifts from the Allfather. And however long they must take mates outside their own kind, these gifts will always breed true."

The first-born of this race was named Volsung, and he was always the first among his brothers and sisters, wisest, strongest and bravest. Within the next few days the remaining eight were born, four male and four female. The brothers of Volsung were Brunar, Gilli, Egil and Kari, and his sisters were Thorhalla, Hallgerd, Rannvieg and Sigvier. They were brought before the Wanderer one night as he sat beside the fire, and he looked upon them and named them. A few days later he called the wolves together and gave them his final instructions, and he promised to return in a year. That night he departed again, although none saw him go.

• • •

When spring came again the cubs were hardly to be
restrained, running and chasing through the woods with
such unlimited vigor that the entire pack was hard put to
keep up with them. In growth they had a head start on
other cubs, but afterward they grew more slowly. By the
end of their first year they were still little more than cubs,
while the true wolves born the same year as themselves
were now nearly adult.

The Wanderer returned to them that same autumn, and
taking the wolflings alone into the forest, he taught them
the secret for changing their shape. It was a trick that they
accomplished easily enough but which brought them no
delight, for they were impatient with the limitations of
their mortal forms. They were, however, only superficially
human in shape, for they still possessed gray eyes and
thick gray manes that extended down to the base of their
spines, with the small wiry frames and pointed ears of
elves. But the Wanderer was pleased, for they were all that
he had meant them to be. Roskva dressed them in clothes
that she had brought, which was not at all to their liking.

Then the Wanderer introduced them to another that he
had brought, Thjalfi, the wood-elf and brother of Roskva,
to assist her in teaching them the ways and weapons of
men and elves. Afterward the Wanderer returned to them
seldom and never stayed for very long, sometimes only
part of a day, coming unexpectantly and leaving again
without a word. But now he came only in the form of an
old man. Indeed he looked more like a wizard from some
ancient tale, wearing a long cloak of dark blue and a hat
that was very broad in the brim and leaning upon a spear
as though it was a staff. He never showed himself clearly,
but at times the wolves could perceive the image of a face
that frightened them. It was a face not as old as they had
thought that was stern and commanding. One eye was

covered, and he wore a patch over his bad eye when he ran as a wolf. Then he seemed to them more a warrior than a wizard, a wolf on the hunt no matter what form he wore.

Thus the years passed, and the Children of the Wanderer prospered. When they reached their tenth year, Thjalfi divided them into three groups of three and took them one group at a time outside the forest of the Vargarbraut. By this time they were beginning to grow swiftly toward adulthood, and they possessed both the size and the experience of those who were five years or more their elders. But there was one thing that they had never seen, raised as they were by wolves and elves, and that was a true human. Now, in accordance with the Wanderer's directions, Thjalfi meant to take them out of the forest to spy upon one of the river holdings, so that they might see how men lived.

In the first group Thjalfi took those who were the best hunters, the quickest and the quietest, for they had to spy out the way and would be the least likely to fall into trouble. Therefore, he took with him Volsung, eldest and first among his brothers and sisters, and Kari the swift and lastly Rannvieg, who was quicker and more deadly with the bow than any of her brothers save one.

Thjalfi led them up the river, the surest path to any holding of men in this region, for they depended upon the river for trade. There were no holdings to be found downstream all the way to the coast, and the nearest upriver lay two days' walk from the wolf-caves. That in itself was no problem, but they took more than enough supplies for a journey of four days. Thjalfi was fearful of what they might find, whether this was a holding of honest men or a lair of river pirates. The elf had no way to know, except he feared that most men would shun the dread Myrkdreyma, while pirates would be attracted to the seclusion of such a place.

The elf had to admit that he was fearful of men, whom he had never before seen except for the Einherjar, the tall, silent warriors of Valhalla. The wolflings were fearful as well but also very excited. They were naturally very curious to see these people of whom they were a part, but mostly they were excited by the prospect of the journey itself, of leaving their forest, and the danger and daring. Thjalfi did not have to search deeply to see that, deep within their hearts, they were more wolves than men.

They found the holding easily enough, even though it lay hidden from the river by a narrow fold of hills. Indeed it lay in a deep depression surrounded on almost every side by hills, a small piece of grassy pasture land enclosed by low ridges and patchy stands of trees that were the fringes of the great Vargarbraut. On the far side the forest came down to within a hundred paces of the farmhouse itself, and they took advantage of its cover to steal a closer look.

Thjalfi had no fear of these folk. This was certainly no pirate's lair, and not even a very large holding even as far as this river knew. There was but the single farmhouse, a barn and a smaller shed between the two. No ship of any size lay pulled up on the bank on the far side of the hill, nor had any ever landed there; only a small rowboat lay upside-down under the cover of a bush. Perhaps a dozen people dwelled here, hidden from the world.

At dawn of the following morning they were already in hiding as near to the farmhouse as they could get. People began to come out of the house soon after, going about their morning chores. Thjalfi had been correct in his estimate, for they saw no more than eleven in all, half of those children. They were mostly occupied with the preparing of a large vegetable garden that stood even closer to the woods than the house did.

"Look! Do they live with wolves also?" Rannvieg exclaimed almost as soon as the door of the house opened.

"No, indeed!" Thjalfi laughed quietly. "Those are dogs, not wolves. You can hear them barking; wolves do not. Men fear the animals of the forest and wolves most of all, for wolves hunt in packs to raid their herds and flocks. In fact, they think of wolves as pirates and thieves."

"Then men are more stupid than wolves!" Volsung said with distaste.

"No, but they are no more or less fearful of wolves than wolves are of them," Thjalfi explained. "Only your wolf-kin can speak and are wise enough to overcome their fears. True wolves cannot; they fear, and that served to protect them from their enemies. Men fear as well, but being of a more intelligent kind, they believe that they should not fear, since they are more clever and capable. What they fear, they hate, and they seek to destroy what they fear."

"But wolves run from what they fear and so avoid the danger altogether," Volsung observed. "Wolves do not consider such things and so are wiser still for it."

"As that may be," Thjalfi said. He drew back behind a protective screen of brush and sat back against the trunk of a small tree. "Listen to me well now, my young friends, for the time has come for me to tell you such things as you have never heard. Understand first that you are the children of Odhinn himself, who took the form of a wolf so that he might go secretly into the wild. The purpose of your being is to serve him when others cannot. But it must be of your own free will, for your lives must remain your own. Even I do not know what that purpose might be; I know only that it is very important to him.

"Soon a choice will be offered you. Five years hence Roskva and I will leave you to return to the elfworld, and all the wolves of your pack will go with us. There they will become immortal themselves, and they will sire a new race of speaking wolves to serve the wood-elves. You may go with them if that is your desire, to live as you most want to be, as wolves. Or you will remain here and live as men, to serve the Allfather in his need.''

The three sat for a moment in silence, heads down, and Thjalfi did not have to ask their thoughts. He knew as well as they their true desire.

Volsung looked up at last. ''You are wise. What do you advise?''

''That is not for me to say,'' the elf answered. ''It is very important that the decision remain your own; that was made plain to me. There is great honor in serving the Allfather, or so mortal men would find it, but he will be in no way disappointed if you choose otherwise. I do know that your lives will be happier and more peaceful if you leave this world, for I can foresee that you will never be content as men, and never at peace among them.''

Volsung sat for a moment, considering all that he had heard and weighing his true desire against his sense of duty. He looked up at last. ''I think that we shall stay.''

The years passed swiftly, and soon the wolflings were quite grown. Then the time had come at last for them to decide, for one spring night the Wanderer appeared among them and bade the Great Wolves of the Vargarbraut to prepare themselves for their last long journey in that world. He did not have to tell the wolfings that they must decide whether they would go or stay. But they had little time, for the Wanderer declared that Roskva and Thjalfi should lead the wolves to the proper world-gate in the morning.

That night Volsung went to the Wanderer as he sat alone by his small fire. Volsung was always first among his brothers and sisters and would surely be their leader as either wolves or men. And so he came alone to ask for answers they all wanted.

The Wanderer sat bent over his small fire, looking distracted and rather uncomfortable in the chill night air.

At most times he seemed a kindly but wise old wizard, a warrior at others, but occasionally he would grow in stature both physically and morally until he seemed a great and powerful lord wrapped in the thin guise of an old man's cloak and hat. Then Volsung knew that, whatever else he might be, the Wanderer was surely one of the Allfather's greatest and most capable lieutenants. This night, however, he was only the Wanderer, kindly and understanding.

He looked up as Volsung approached. "Come along, my son. I was wondering when you might show up."

"Master, would you not be more comfortable in wolf form?" Volsung asked.

"I might," the Wanderer replied, poking at his fire with a stick. "But that would hardly be a good example. You gave up your wolf form for me, so I can at least do as much for you. It hardly matters, for I have many forms and none is truly my own. What would you know? Can you not decide?"

"No, I know my choice and I must stay," Volsung replied. "I only wondered why the wolves must leave us. If we face troubled times ahead, then we are stronger with their numbers. Is there some reason why they must go?"

"You know, of course, that there must be," the Wanderer replied and laid his stick in the fire. "Bren Skoggi is old, almost too old for the hunt. Megelna your mother is old as well. Kelan the storyteller departed long ago. If the pack goes now into the elfworld, then they will soon become immortal and grow young and strong again."

"True," the boy agreed. "But there has always been death in this realm. The Allfather cannot save all creatures from the death of age. I think, instead, that there is some advantage to their departure."

The Wanderer nodded slowly. "Good will come in three ways from their going. First for themselves, for they are a noble kind who will soon be gone from this world but will flourish there. Secondly for the elves, who need such swift and capable companions to help protect their forests from the evil things that have been hiding there. And lastly for yourselves, the Children of the Wolves. For if you choose to be wolves, then you must go from this realm and you should be with your own pack. But if you choose to stay, then you must live as men, not wolves, and it will be safer for you if you do not live in the company of wolves who think and speak as men.''

"That is what Thjalfi told us, to beware the fears of men.''

"Then heed his advice, and never let men make you an object to be hated and feared. I wish that it was not so, that men would make better use of their capacity for wisdom. But so it is, and they cannot be changed overnight. You must hide whatever differences exist between yourselves and men.

"Tomorrow, if you remain, you must begin to live as men in every way. I will bring you tools and other things you need, and you will go to the great clearing near the fork of the river and build yourselves a holding with hall and barn. I will bring you cattle and gold to trade for other things and later show you how to build a ship.''

"I will remain," Volsung said emphatically, as if the Wanderer had doubted him personally.

"Oh, I do not question that," the Wanderer replied. "But your brothers and sisters might decide otherwise, for their choice is their own. Nor can I allow only one or two to remain alone. Six at least should remain, for you must be enough to found a race that may have to endure some time before you are needed for your great task. For I can foresee now that it will not be for you but for your descendants many generations removed to serve the Allfather's need. You know, do you not, that you are in truth the son of Odhinn?''

"So we have been told," Volsung replied. "But it has seemed to me for some time that we are no less your children."

"Is that so?" the Wanderer asked in amazement. "You have surprised me indeed! I am glad that my children have one so quick and perceptive to protect them in the infancy of their race. But I trust that you will keep your guesses to yourself."

The boy nodded gravely. "Odhinn is our father, and you are our guardian. That is all anyone should know."

"That is best. For I shall always come to you in your need, to help you either directly or indirectly. But if the truth was known, then my coming and going would be marked and my purpose defeated."

Volsung sat in silence for a moment, then rose slowly as if to leave. The Wanderer glanced up at him. "No more questions?"

"I guess not," Volsung replied. "Except . . . what will you do if we choose to go?"

The Wanderer shrugged. "I will simply try again, although with some subtle differences. If the Children of the Wolves were raised by men, then they might be more willing to remain men. But I do not want you to worry about it."

"You gave us life," Volsung pointed out.

"But your lives remain your own. Live them as you wish. I will be pleased if you stay, but I will be equally pleased if you go. Yes, I brought you into existence to be my tools in my time of need, but your futures belong to you, and I wish you happiness. I made a mistake fifteen years ago that I shall not repeat."

"A mistake?" Volsung asked.

"Yes, and a most annoying one at that!" The Wanderer laughed. "I brought nine children into this world, the best that I could want, and as their father I love them."

CHAPTER THREE

When morning came the wolves were eager to be on their way, for Roskva and Thjalfi had told them much about the elf-world. They were filled with wonder and delight by the thought of a world that was all deep, green forests and tall mountains, swift rivers and icy lakes. Where they need not live in fear of men, but with the companionship of elves. Unlike men, they were little impressed with thoughts of immortality. Forests and game meant the most to them, and a warm house with a fire during the winter's snows. The elf-world promised all they could want or need.

That was even more true for the Children of the Wolves, for it offered them a chance to be what they wanted, content and free from worry. Here they faced only fear and uncertainty, in constant danger from a kind they had no wish to claim as their own. And yet they also possessed the better qualities of their human forms, a sense of loyalty and obligation, and a desire to do good. And, above all, a need to face a challenge and overcome it and somehow be better themselves, more worthy of the Allfather's trust, by doing it. And so it was, when the pack made ready for the long journey to the hidden world-gate, the wolflings sat apart with the Wanderer and watched.

The wolves kept apart and watched their children fearfully. Even after they had been given speech, they feared to say the wrong thing and found that words often fell short. Bren Skoggi and his mate Megelna went over at last to speak for them all, for Bren had been the leader of their pack since the time before, and Megelna was wisest of them all. Words seldom escaped her.

"It seems that we have come to the parting of our trails," Bren said. "Out of respect for the Allfather and the great task that awaits you, I will not ask you to come with us. But because you are dear to us, I will not ask you to remain. Your path is your own, for you to choose as you feel you must."

"That is so," Megelna agreed. "My only hope is that wherever your path may lead and to whatever task awaits you, it might one day lead you back to us. Then we will hunt and play again in the forests of the elf-world."

"And yet that cannot be," the Wanderer said. "For they must take their mates among mortal men and women. Nor do I see any swift completion of their task. I fear that being mortal, they will grow old and die before the proper time has come, and the task they await will fall to the children of their children. They serve only to keep their race alive and strong until the time does come. They must understand that, or else I advise them to follow you now. That is why they were offered the choice, so that they might pledge their lives willingly."

"And how long will that be?" Megelna asked. "For are they not also the Allfather's own children and themselves immortal?"

"That was not the plan in their making. However. . . ." The Wanderer paused and looked up at Volsung intently for a long moment. At last he sat back and laughed. "Melgelna is clever indeed! They are the children of the

Allfather and possessed of spirits of power as other servants of Asgardh rather than mortal souls.''

He sat for a long moment, deep in thought, before looking up. ''Very well. Hear now the second choice of the Children of the Wolves. For those whose lot it is to wait, they are free, after their own children are grown, to follow the pack into the elf-world to live a new life as wolves. For I will come to them from time to time and will lead them to the world-gate. And for those who die or are slain, the Valkyries will take them not to Valhalla but to join their pack in the undying realm. That shall be the Allfather's promise to the Children of the Wolves for as long as their race endures.''

''Then we will be free to go without the burden of sorrow and guilt,'' Megelna said.

''And we shall also find it much easier to stay,'' Volsung added. ''We are willing to give our lives to the Allfather's task, but this makes our choice a simpler one.''

''Stay or go, it is time for you to make that choice,'' the Wanderer said, rising. ''It is quite a long walk to the world-gate, so be on your way if you hope to be there by tomorrow night. You must pass through the lands of men, and there are terrible beasts in the wild at night.''

Bren lifted his ears. ''What manner of beasts?''

''Wolves!'' the Wanderer declared. ''Elf, show them the way home!''

They built their hall in a large clearing near the river, just above the Hronn's junction with a lesser stream that wound its way up from the south. The only place suitable was well away from the heart of the forest and on the far side of the river as well. The Children of the Wolves complained on both accounts, claiming that there was no room to run and hunt, and the river separated them from their caves. Of course, the Wanderer took no notice of that. He was not pleased with the prospect of allowing them to remain in the forest at all. Other folk would think them strange enough, dwelling in the Myrkdreyma where few men dared even to go. But if trouble did come upon them unexpectedly, then he thought it best that they should be in the woods, where they possessed every advantage, to fight or flee as they must.

Building a hall as the Wanderer taught them was no easy task, with the laying of stone and the cutting of wood. They had strength enough for the task but little patience for this type of work, appallingly unexciting compared to hunting and tracking. Moreover, they could not understand why they simply could not continue to live as they had, dwelling in the wolf-caves and hunting for their food.

"It makes no sense to me," Brunar, the laziest, complained. "This house you have had us make is nothing more than the inside of a cave pulled out into the open. Building a house for animals is even more foolish. These cattle and goats are under the terribly mistaken impression that we are here only to provide for their every need. It is cruel to mislead them so and silly to have to care for them when we can hunt for all we need."

"It might seem foolish to you," the Wanderer said, peevishly, his patience wearing thin. "Yes, you can live in the forest more easily. But you must at least pretend to be like other men. Also, you must soon take mates from among mortal men and women. They will certainly have to tolerate a great deal of your strange ways, but they will at least expect a house."

"Then I am not sure that I want to have them," Egil said, speaking for them all. "They sound like the most trouble of all. Wolves are easier to deal with."

"Well, I cannot have you marrying wolves!" the Wanderer declared. "Then your children would be true wolves, and of no use to me. Either do as I have told you, or I will show you to the world-gate right now, and we will all be happier!''

They built their hall and barn as the Wanderer showed them, with stone fences to hold the small herd of cattle and goats he brought for them. And he taught them to garden, which was even less to their liking. A large part of the problem was that the Wanderer had to be away much more often than not and could remain only a few days at a time. He often returned to find that they had made very little progress in their tasks or had forgotten what he had told them. In many ways they were still children with very little patience for what did not interest them.

When they had completed their holding, after two and a half years of work, he showed them how to make a small ship of their own, and it took them only three tries to build one that was fairly seaworthy. Teaching them to sail, however, was another matter entirely. Wolves had no liking for the open water, and the Children of the Wolves possessed that instinct as well. Of them all, only Kari and Rannvieg ever learned the feel of wind and waves well enough to be trusted with the tiller. Except for Gilli, who became sick from the motion very quickly, the others could at least row.

Five years after the departure of the wolves, Odhinn decided that his children were ready to meet the world of men and take their mates. He returned to them in the spring, at a time when a great festival was to be held in one of the larger holdings of the Rhine valley. He was to accompany them to the festival himself under the pretext that he was their father and the lord of their holding, and he would arrange as many marriages as he could. It went against his dignity, this role of matchmaker for a pack of

half-wolves, but he bore it with good grace. He did not
trust anyone else to do it right.

They made their little ship ready to sail and loaded it
with their cargo of cheese. When the Wanderer had brought
them cattle, he had taught them how to make cheese from
the milk they did not use. Now the wolflings loved cheese
above all else. Also they possessed a herd of dairy cattle
several times beyond what they required, and being of the
wild, they could not bear to see food go to waste. Therefore, they had begun to make large round cheeses at a
furious pace. When the Wanderer discovered this he was
amazed beyond words, for in five years they had accumu-
lated enough cheese to feed every wolf in the northlands
through a long winter.

"I have done all that I can to get you ready for this," he
told them after they had landed their ship at the festival
with all the grace of a dying whale. "Do not be afraid.
These are only men and women, and little different from
yourselves. Choose your potential mates as best you can; I
think those qualities which will attract you will serve you
best. But, above all else, be polite. I have told you all that
I can about this matter."

He caught their vacant stares and stared back in surprise. "Have I not spoken with you on such matters as
. . . mating? No? At least the elves have told you about
such things." He paused, realizing that he should have
known better. He threw up his arms in hopelessness and
turned away. "Worthless elves! Do the best you can.
Work whatever charms you have, and I will do the rest."

The wolflings were charming enough, at least to other
wolves. They were also graced by fortune far more than
they desired, and each was able to come up with a potential suitor before long. Then the Wanderer, using the most
subtle magic at his command and even more subtle politi-
cal dealings, would bicker, plead or bribe marriages out of

nine hesitant fathers. He also managed to turn a handsome profit from their cargo of cheese while he was at it. Whatever else the world of men might have thought of the Children of the Wolves, they made inarguably the best cheese in the mortal realm.

"Cheese!" Odhinn muttered into his beard. "I need a hero, and I get cheese-makers!"

He also had to work some less subtle magic on their perspective mates. Any mortal would have balked at the thought of marrying a shape-changer, but these young men and women also faced the difficulty of having children who would be born as wolves and live their entire first year in furred form. That was a secret that could hardly be kept from them, unfortunately, but also one that had to be guarded from all the rest of the world. Odhinn employed his best magic to the task, for it was very important that they not only know and accept the truth but also keep their mouths firmly closed on the subject. He never did allow the wolflings to know what he was forced to do for them, and he also got the entire group away from the festival as soon as their business was complete.

The Wanderer was away again almost as soon as he got them safely home. More worlds than Midhgardh had grown steadily darker in the years since the finding of the ring, and Odhinn could no longer spare his children any more of his time. Great dragons were harassing the dwarves ceaselessly, the only creatures powerful enough to tear open the gates of their hidden cities. And the elves were constantly raided by both trolls and their own evil counterparts. Utgardh-Loki had almost completely secured his own authority among the darker kindreds and now took the liberty of engaging his enemy with the lesser races under his control, sparing his own people.

Odhinn arranged his defenses as best he could, concentrating first on locating and securing the lesser world-gates. The Aesir no longer possessed the power to destroy more than just a very few of the gates they had carelessly opened long ages past in innocent, less dangerous days. If they could secure the world-gates, either by force or some physical barrier, then most of the evil creatures would be contained within their own worlds. Deprived of other peoples to raid and loot, many of the evil races, Jotnar, the dark elves and trolls, would cease to flourish and even turn upon each other as prey. And some day, aided by the power of the ring, Odhinn hoped to pursue such creatures to destruction in their own worlds.

Another year passed swiftly. Now the holding in the middle of the Vargarbraut seemed more like a place alive, and the wolflings first began to emerge from beneath the sorrow and loneliness of the lives that they had chosen for themselves. So long as they had only wolves for company, that was all they knew or wanted to be. Now they began to see what it was really like to live as men. It was not so bad as they had anticipated, for now they had others to show them small things of interest and find some pleasure in a way of life they had thought bland and unexciting.

Before the end of the first year, they began to have children of their own. The first to be born was Rerir, son of Volsung and his mortal mate Hildigunn. As the Wanderer had said, Rerir was born in the shape of a wolf, as all true children of their race would be, and he would not be able to take human form until the end of his first year. The mortal folk who had married into their clan had been prepared and were not surprised, but they did see for the first time the danger that this could bring upon them all if it were known.

By the coming spring three others were born, all in wolfish form. During the past year the Children of the Wolves had traveled up and down the river at times, selling their cheeses and smoked meats for the things they needed but could not make. In this way they became known to others who lived along the river, and came to be held in suspicion and fear. It was enough that they dwelled in Myrkdreyma, the forest of evil, but all those who met them could sense something strange about them. They were small of stature, quiet and shy, but men who spoke with them came to feel as though they faced mighty warriors or noble kings, great ones who instilled awe and respect in lesser men. But animals felt only fear; horses would not bear them, and dogs barked and howled but always kept their distance.

It was also in the spring of that year that someone dared to seek out the holding of the Children of the Wolves for the first time. He was Sigarr, son of Arnor the Bold, the lord of the greatest holding along the entire length of the river Hronn. It was not by accident that he was also the father of Hildigunn, mate of Volsung, and yet they were unlike in every way. Hildigunn was quick, bright and pleasant, while her father was cold and calculating, greedy and given to quick temper. He wrestled wealth from a land where few men could find it; he kept pirates out of the Hronn by the strength of his fleet of quick ships, lying in wait at his holding at the river's mouth. But he kept their plundered cargoes as his own and also took tribute from other lordlings of the river.

Sigarr Arnorsson had given both his daughter and his sister's son into the deal. Neither were eldest, and so of little worth to him. Like the others who had pledged their children for marriage, he had known from the start that there was something strange about the deal. If nothing came of it, then he had lost little. But if there was indeed something to be had of it, then he intended to get what he could, whether by gift, by theft, or if need be by murder. He came now to discover what he could of this strange clan, and how he might profit from them. His excuse was that he came hoping to find a new grandchild.

That in itself was trouble enough for the wolflings. Sigarr did indeed have a grandson, and his sister's son had a daughter as well, but it would be some months before either would be able to take human form.

Sigarr came one bright morning, bearing with him a score of his finest warriors in his largest ship. He arrived unexpectedly and unannounced, and the wolflings did not know what to make of it. At least their mortal mates were quicker of thought in this matter, and they hid their wolf-ish children the moment they saw the ship push ashore. And when Hildigunn saw her father aboard that ship, she had all their weapons made ready.

Volsung was there to meet him at the shore and treated him as best he could. Sigarr feigned complete amiability, asking only to see any grandchild he might have. Hildigunn was there as quick as she could, and hearing this story, she was doubtful. The only solution seemed to be to reveal to Sigarr the truth and hope that he would serve Odhinn's will by keeping silent. Hildigunn doubted that, but she could see no alternative short of slaying any visitor who came to call. They could at least try.

Therefore, they took Sigarr into the hall and explained the matter as plainly and as attractively as they might. They lacked the Wanderer's special persuasiveness, but at first Sigarr was at least willing to listen. But when Hildigunn brought in her son, Sigarr drew back in alarm and would have nothing more to do with the matter.

"Any fool can see the evil in this!" he declared. "All wolves are creatures of darkness, and the great wolves of the Myrkdreyma are evil spirits in living form!"

"The wolves of the Vargarbraut are wise and gentle," Volsung answered hotly. "The Wanderer called them the most noble of animals, the lords of the forest."

"The Wanderer!" Sigarr said contemptuously. "I remember that old wizard, and I thought him strange and evil at the time."

With that he turned and marched from the hall and immediately called his men to arms. But the Children of the Wolves and their mates needed no more warning than that. Bowstrings snapped, and sixteen of Sigarr's warriors who had been reaching for their weapons suddenly found their sword hands pierced with arrows. They all stood motionless, not daring to move, for in that same instant the bows were reloaded and readied.

Sigarr himself felt the point of two knives in his back. Whether or not Volsung would have been so quick to use his knife, Sigarr knew that his daughter held the other and that she would not hesitate.

"I suppose that it is safe enough to let you go," Volsung said in his ear. "Sixteen of your warriors will never draw a bow or hold a sword again, not with their former strength. I would require an oath of you, if I thought your word was worth that much. I hope that one warning is enough."

Sigarr boarded his ship and left quickly enough, although he had to trust his vessel to the river's swift current now that he did not have enough men to row. He lacked the courage to remain where he was at such an obvious disadvantage. Hildigunn, who knew her father best, would not willingly let him go. But the wolflings did not understand war or murder, and they could not begin to comprehend why anyone would wish them harm if there was nothing to gain by it.

As soon as Sigarr returned home, he began to plot how he might destroy the Children of the Wolves. Volsung was correct in one thing. His sixteen wounded warriors had lost the use of their best hand, leaving them unable to hold a sword or draw a strong bow. Also he had seen at least a part of the fighting skills that not only the wolflings but their mortal mates possessed, and he saw that only a large force would be able to overpower them in battle. He knew also that he did not want to meet them in a fair fight with any force of arms.

A little after a month of his first visit to the Children of the Wolves, Sigarr returned with as large an army as he could muster. His plan was to come veiled in the growing shadows of twilight, quietly and unseen, and take his prey by complete surprise. He hoped to shoot them unaware with arrows, or as many as he might, then hunt down and trap the others as he could. It seemed to him a good plan, for they were too few to post a watch out, and there were no others about who could give warning.

But that was a thing that was not so easily done, with nearly two hundred and fifty warriors in eleven creaking, old ships. Moreover all of Sigarr's men were superstitious of the forest and the tales of dark and terrible creatures, tales that Sigarr had happily recited to win their support earlier. And they were as afraid of the Children of the Wolves, having heard how they had disabled a score of Sigarr's best warriors, and Sigarr had added to that with many evil lies. They did not know what manner of beings they faced, mortal or demon, and they were hesitant and afraid. Thus the wolflings heard them as they came ashore, and so had some small time to prepare.

Sigarr circled his men completely about the wolfling hall, then closed his net quickly and quietly so that none within might escape. They walked cautiously with sword or spear ready and bows drawn, fearful of what they might face and anticipating anything. The holding might be full of dragons or monstrous wolves the size of horses, according to Sigarr's tales. Many suspected that dragons or other creatures were stealing up behind them, ready to trap the trappers.

They emerged from the forest at last, surrounding the

holding. The barn door stood open, but the hall itself was completely closed, its doors and windows tightly shut. Light escaped through cracks in the shutters, and a trail of gray smoke rose from the chimney into the night air, but those were the only signs that anyone was about. Sigarr stood for a moment, watching the hall and wondering if the Children of the Wolves were there or had escaped his trap. The appearance of the hall, as if under siege, argued that they were within.

He drew his sword and stepped out into the open. "Volsung! Come on out now, or we will burn you out!"

There was no response, but Volsung was indeed watching him through a crack in the shutters. He and Brunar had seen the ships landing in the darkness and had run back to the hall to collect the others, only to find their escape cut off. Now he measured the strength of his enemy and wondered what he might do. Finding himself in such a trap grated against his wolfish instinct, and he wanted to run and howl. But he had only one priority, and that was to get his people away safely.

Volsung knew what Sigarr meant to do; it was a common tactic when river lordlings fought among themselves. But he did not intend to find himself trapped in that way. He had remembered the warnings of Thjalfi the elf, and those were lessons that he had learned better than his teacher had anticipated. Perhaps it was true that it was better to meet an enemy in the open than to be burned in the house, but it was also wise to know when it was time to run. And wisest of all to anticipate such an escape. The wolflings had not trusted houses from the start, and they had built into their own an unseen way out to the safety of the forest should they ever have to retreat.

"Hildigunn," he said, turning quickly to the others gathered behind him, "you take the mortal folk and the cubs and go. Make the ship ready for a long journey. Kari, you go ahead and see that the way is clear, then move quietly along the shore and set a torch to each of their ships. We will not be followed.''

"And the rest of you?" Hildigunn asked.

"We will keep them busy for a few minutes, then follow," he replied. "Just have the ship ready as quickly as you can. Now go."

Kari had already pulled aside a large wooden chest, revealing the dark opening of a tunnel in the floor. Taking a small torch, he climbed inside. The mortal folk followed quickly, carrying the four young cubs with them, and Volsung slid the chest back in place when they were gone. Then the wolflings took their bows and went one each to a window of the hall.

"Volsung, this is your last warning!" Sigarr called again.

Volsung still did not respond, and Sigarr waited no longer. At his direction a handful of warriors approached the hall cautiously, each bearing a flaming torch. Bowstrings snapped and arrows shot from unseen openings, each shaft finding one of the advancing warriors. The wolflings did not defer to kindness or compassion; this time they shot to kill, and with terrible accuracy. But Sigarr knew now that they were indeed inside. Arrows flew in return, only to strike harmless against closed shutters.

Now Sigarr began to send in more warriors with torches, as stealthily as they could, under the cover of his own archers. But that hardly made any difference, for the wolflings were able to shoot out effectively without opening the shutters. They were able to make their hall a fortress, but only for a time. Eventually a few of the quickest—and luckiest—warriors were able to come near enough to throw their brands up onto the roof. But even that proved to be of little effect, for the roof was not thatched but planked. It would burn as well as a thatched roof, but it was much slower to kindle. That bought the Children of the Wolves even more time, and their attackers were now so preoccupied that they did not even notice their own ships blazing on the shore.

When Volsung heard the torches thump against the wooden roof, he called the defenders together in the main room. They calmly put away their weapons, and six immense gray wolves abruptly appeared in their place. By now Sigarr and a group of his warriors had advanced on the main door, encouraged by the cessation of the steady barrage of deadly arrows. Most of the attackers stood gathered about the hall, piling their torches on the wooden roof to encourage it to blaze.

Sigarr kicked open the unbarred door, and almost at the same instant, a huge gray wolf shot out the door, bearing him down with its great weight. Other wolves streaked out through the crowd of startled men, seemingly scores of wolves in the confusion, each twice the size of any they had ever seen. They scattered in terror, and the wolves ran past them into the forest beyond.

The attackers drew their weapons and turned to follow, and it was then that they discovered their ships were in flames. In rage they cursed and shot wild, unsure of their targets in the shadows of the night forest. The wolves paid them no heed, racing with heads low to the shore where a small ship stood ready, sail spread to the wind as it glided past on the swift current. The wolves ran out along a small point of land and leaped as far as they could, hurtling nearly thirty feet before they came down in the river with heavy splashes. They quickly swam out to the ship and were safely aboard before anyone on shore had a chance to find their range.

CHAPTER FOUR

Volsung pulled himself up over the side of the ship, eager hands lifting him by the shoulders, and converted back to human form before he slipped to the deck. Other wolflings were coming over the side as quickly as they could be pulled in, while the little ship pitched and drifted unattended down the river. He paused for a moment to check quickly, and everyone seemed to be present. All the mortal folk were there, and the wolves were coming aboard. Even the cubs sat beneath the overhanging rear deck.

Fires lined the shore for some distance. There was a line of torches along the water's edge immediately across from them as archers stood watching their prey escape. But the greatest fires were those that were rapidly consuming the seven longboats pulled up along the bank some half a mile behind. Farther back in the forest, the roof of the hall was now beginning to burn furiously.

Arrows suddenly shot out of the darkness. Most passed harmlessly overhead, while others fell short. Two came down uncomfortably close to Rannvieg, the one wolf remaining in the water. One hit the water just short of her haunch, while the other stuck in the planks to one side of her head. She snapped viciously at the shaft, paused to look about nervously, then leaped up to catch the side of the ship with her forelegs. She was hauled in so quickly that she tumbled over the gunwale on top of her rescuers, scattering people and wet wolves across the deck. Then everyone huddled in close against the inside of the hull, causing the ship to list pronouncedly, to wait until they had drifted out of range.

Volsung at least had more sense. He retreated to the stern and steered the little ship as far as he dared to the opposite shore. The others, seeing what he was doing, took the oars to propel the ship more swiftly down the river. But the danger was quickly past. After a few minutes they put away the oars, for the river was too treacherous at night to navigate with any speed. Volsung turned the tiller over to Rannvieg and set Kari to watch the sail.

"Now what?" Hildigunn asked. "Where can we go that this will not happen again?"

"North," Volsung replied, for he had already considered that. "Beyond the Hafvang, to the lands of mountains and deep valleys."

They all looked up in surprise.

"Why there?" Brunar asked.

"Because few men live in that land," Volsung explained. "Their holdings are far apart. We need never have dealings with them, and from now on we, or our children, will have to travel far to find mates. There we shall remain until our duty to the Allfather is fulfilled, or until our numbers grow to the point that none may threaten us."

"But will the Wanderer know where we have gone?" Kari asked.

Volsung smiled. "That I do not doubt."

The deed did not long go unnoticed by the Lord of Asgardh.

Brynhild the Valkyrie was not far away when the attack on the Children of the Wolves came, passing over the northlands on her nightly rounds. At once she sensed the presence of battle and the nearness of death, and she turned from her course to investigate, wondering if some valiant warrior might die that night whose spirit would be worth taking. Such an occasion came seldomly, even in Midhgardh. Valiant men were few, and they were most often the ones who survived their battles.

But as Brynhild came nearer, she knew that something was wrong. She alone knew anything of Odhinn's secret, for these were lands she patrolled every night and little happened that she was unaware of. She knew that the Lord of Asgardh came here often and that the ones who dwelled in the forest were under his protection. Just what they meant to him was something she did not know. But if they were in trouble, then she believed that she should do something to help them. Odhinn's true will was her duty, whether or not his orders were direct.

She rode in low over the river, still invisible to the mortal eye, and there she saw the wolflings making good their escape. Relieved, she passed on up the river to do what she could to delay pursuit. It seemed that her help was not greatly needed; half the forest appeared to be in flames.

Sigarr sat uneasily upon an upended crate, watching the confusion about him. The wolflings had escaped, he was sure of that. He wondered if they had had the upper hand, facing an army of two hundred and fifty and getting away unharmed. Nearly sixty warriors were dead or wounded from their arrows, and seven ships—four of those his own—were destroyed. Sigarr himself was nursing cracked ribs he had received when that monstrous wolf, perhaps Volsung himself, had born him down. And now he faced a long walk home.

A startled shout caught his attention, and he turned to see what could have brought instant silence to this confused crowd. There, above the center of the holding, hovered a Valkyrie, a small figure in white armor and a deep blue cape astride a powerful horse that shifted and pranced in midair, all clearly illuminated in the light of the flames. Could there have been a surer sign of the rightness of his act? Even in failure, the gods blessed his deed. He stepped forward to face the mysterious rider.

The Valkyrie lowered her long spear until it pointed directly at him.

"Mortal, do you claim responsibility for this act?" Her voice echoed forcefully through the night.

Sigarr drew his sword and held it up to her in salute. "I do!"

"Then you shall pay for this evil deed!"

A bolt of lightning shot from her spear to envelope him, and in a flash of blinding light, he was gone. The Valkyrie paused for a moment, as if searching the crowd for other guilty members, then turned her horse and rode away into the night. But her warning was plain. No one there would dare to pursue the Children of the Wolves or ever raise weapon against them again for fear of incurring the same swift punishment.

The long passage across the northern sea was not an easy one, even in the gentle days of spring. Their ship was small and light and easy for them to manage, but it was too small for as many as were now forced to dwell on it. Moreover, they were very ill-prepared. There were skins of fresh water, but for provisions they had only some cheese and dried meat, barely enough for two days. So it was that they were forced to come ashore often to hunt.

In time they came to Vikfjallaland, and they began to search about for a place to make their home. In a deep fjord they found a swift river, and they sailed up it as far as they could, more than fifty miles from the open sea. They left their ship in a sheltered bend of the river and climbed higher still into the towering peaks of rock and ice. The forest there was thick, deep and silent, so that the wolflings felt very much at home. Volsung thought that they were safe at last, and so they selected a small clearing in the forest of the gentler slopes and made their new home.

At first their life was not easy. They had no provisions and few tools, so the work on their new home was very slow. They all worked when they could, but the wolflings had to provide for them by hunting, since the only food they had was what they could catch. But they were not so badly off as others would have been; the forest remained their home, and they would have had an easy life if they had not had cubs and mortal mates to provide for.

Their hardship was soon over, however, for the Wanderer returned to them as quickly as he could. He brought with him all the things they needed most, tools and arrows, cloth to make clothes and rope and also a small herd of cattle. But first he lined them up and took a long, hard look at each of them, until at last he seemed satisfied that no harm had come to them. Then he took a second hard look at the cubs.

"Are you pleased with the little ones?" Volsung asked at last.

"No, I am not pleased with the little ones," the Wanderer replied testily. "Why is it that I see only four? I want to see more! Whole packs of little wolves!"

Rannvieg laughed aloud. "Give us time!"

He turned on her swiftly. "You are pregnant. And I suppose that you were in the middle of that fight?"

Rannvieg shrugged; this was news to her. "In fact, I nearly missed the boat."

"What does it matter?" Volsung asked. "You said that the Allfather requires only one of us when the time comes."

"That is true enough. But I am concerned that you will not be here when you are needed." He laid aside his spear and sat down wearily on a cut log. "Your race must be strong if you are to survive. This world is a meaner place than you anticipated . . . than I anticipated. I made a mistake, and you were able to escape only by your own resourcefulness."

"What do we do now?" Volsung asked.

"You seem to have found your own answer to that," the Wanderer replied. "Do as you have planned. Live in peace, and I will do what I can for you. Danger cannot come upon you as swiftly here, so the Valkyries will be able to watch over you now."

Volsung nodded. "Then we shall stay here. What is a Valkyrie?"

The Wanderer sighed in exasperation. "Valkyries are immortal maidens who wear armor, carry spears and ride their horses through the night sky. Any one of them can slay the fiercest dragon, and all of them are entirely too presumptuous. The one watching over you is a special terror."

"Oh. Then why can they not perform the Allfather's great task?"

"There is a simple explanation for that," the Wanderer said as he rose and took up his spear. "It is, however, none of your business."

The Wanderer left them soon, and from that time on he came only very seldom. The Children of the Wolves never questioned aloud what duties kept him from them, often for years at a time. But from the time of his first visit to them in the northlands, they were watched over closely.

Every night Brynhild passed over their holding, making herself visible so that those who watched could see her.

The wolflings prospered in the years that followed. They were too resourceful to be hampered long by adversity, and like their parent race, they did not dwell on their misfortunes but faced each new day as a time separate and distinct from the past. Their race also prospered as the Wanderer had wished. Thirty-two were born in their second generation. And all were wolflings, born as wolf cubs. Rerir, son of Volsung, grew up to be in most ways like his father but with the patience and wisdom of his mortal mother. Everyone thought that he would be their likely leader after his father; like wolves, leadership among them went to the one most capable, as decided by the whole pack. When he and many of his generation came of age, the Wanderer returned and took them by ship far to the south, and they returned many days later with mortal mates of their own. But the next generation, he said, they would be able to take mates from among their own kind. Being of wolfish descent, they were much more free than men to inbreed.

Soon after, Hildigunn, the mate of Volsung, died suddenly. Everyone was shocked by this, and not just because it had come so suddenly. Hildigunn was, of course, of mortal lineage, not a wolfling, but she was the first of their clan to go. The Children of the Wolves were dismayed, for this forced upon them many questions that they found disquieting. But Volsung's miseries were his own, and he sat dejected, his face turned from the promise of life, for this was a grief that his kind could not lightly lay aside.

The Wanderer came to them as soon as he could. He took the Children of the Wolves, the original nine wolflings, and spoke to them and their mates alone in the main hall. Of his own generation, only Rerir was allowed to attend.

"I do not know what I might say," he told them. "Life can be both kind and cruel; the future does not shape itself, nor does chance strike where it will. I have no answers; perhaps you are not even certain what questions you might ask. I cannot bring Hildigunn back to you. She is gone now from any realm into which the Allfather's powers extend. What then can I offer you?"

Volsung sat for a long moment, looking down. "I want to leave this life. I want to go now into the elf-world, as you promised, to rejoin my pack and be what I have always desired to be. Rerir has come into his prime, and in some ways he is wiser than myself. Let him lead the wolflings now."

"Do you seek to run away from this life and forget the time that you have shared with Hildigunn so that her memory will not trouble you?"

Volsung shook his head firmly. "No. But there is nothing more in this life to interest me. I want to take my memories and go now, while they are still fresh. My future is not here, only my past."

The Wanderer sat for a moment and considered that. "You could not have given me a fairer answer. I do not see how I can refuse it. But what of the rest of you? I can see that all of you are nearly as troubled. What would you ask of me?"

"My lord," Rannvieg began hesitantly, "we have realized that we do not appear to grow old, while our mates do."

"You know that your sire was the Allfather in the form of a great wolf," the Wanderer said. "From him you received the ability of shape-changing. You know also that you have received a measure of immortality. You ceased to age more than twenty years ago. You received lastly the promise that when your children were grown and ready to carry on in your place, then you would be free to go."

The Wanderer departed almost as soon as he had come, going again with the rising of the morning sun. With him went Volsung, who smiled as he made his farewells as though the weight he bore was already beginning to lift. But he went alone, for all the others felt that their own time had not yet come. He did not begrudge them that happiness, and they did not fault him his choice. But it was still a sad parting, that one of the nine should have to go before the rest.

Volsung kept his mortal form for a while, for he did not want to tempt those who remained behind. But they had not gone far, and he was just about to shift into his wolf form, when a strange horse stepped out of the bushes into the middle of the path. It was the most unusual horse that Volsung had ever seen, for it was immense, and it had eight legs. He stopped and stared, and the horse stared back.

"Hello, sleepy," the Wanderer said as he stepped up to the horse. He set aside his broad-brimmed hat and gray wizard's robe to reveal the armor of some strange type that he wore beneath. He folded away his robe and pulled himself into the horse's saddle. Or rather the front saddle; this beast wore a second farther back.

"Come along," he said when Volsung did not move. "It is a journey of many days to the hidden gate into the elf-world, but Sleipnir will have us there in half an hour."

"But he has eight legs!" Volsung said in dismay.

Sleipnir snorted contemptuously, as horses can do very well. "So what? You smell like a wolf!"

Early in the spring of the following year, Rerir returned to the old holding in the forest of the Vargarbraut. He took with him the older wolflings and half the warriors of his own generation. After two decades there was little remaining of the former holding but the burnt-out walls of the old hall. They quickly restored the old hall for their immediate use, then spent the spring and summer building new halls to accommodate their greatly increased numbers. Then, in the later part of the summer, before the coming of the autumn's storms, they returned in their ships to the northern lands to bring the rest of their clan to the holding in the Vargarbraut.

The prosperity of the wolflings continued unbroken, and they knew only peace and contentment. The Wanderer still returned from time to time to help the younger wolflings find mates or to lead their elders into the elf-world. But he soon found that they could find mates of their own, for the lordlings of the northlands now knew who they were and willingly gave their sons and daughters in marriage. In those days the wolflings came to be known among mortal men as the Volsungs after the first chieftain of their clan.

In that time Loki had been many years among the elves, aiding them as he could in their ceaseless fight with the evil things that had invaded their forests. He had only just returned, bearing the praises of the elf-king, Alflysa, for the gift of the Great Wolves. Small though their number still was, they had done much in assisting the wood-elves in their fight.

"They are also trying to close the world-gates . . . at least the lesser ones," Loki added.

Odhinn looked up from reading the elf-king's message. "Now that is a surprise."

"Well, not actually close," Loki ammended. "They just want to put locks on the gates, if you understand what I mean, rendering them impassable to anyone but themselves and the Aesir."

Loki paused then and looked around. "Someone is coming."

Odhinn felt it also, an incredible surge of unseen power. The Aesir had once felt like that in their approach, before they had restrained their powers to take physical form. Now there were but few in the nine realms who possessed such power. Odhinn stilled a sudden surge of panic. Unless the Fenris Wolf broke his chain or Surtur escaped the imprisonment of his own realm, there was only one being in existance who could cause the Allfather to fear for himself.

"Go!" he declared, taking Loki by the arm and thrusting him forward. And for once Loki did not argue; he knew as well who it was and wanted no part of it. But he did not go far.

Odhinn turned, carefully composed, to face Jordh as she began to materialize before him. This time she did not project just an invisible extension of herself but came in all her power, still tied by a slender thread to the world that gave her existence. This time she meant business.

"So you have returned," Odhinn said. "It has been many long years since we last met."

"Many years," Jordh agreed. "And you have cautiously avoided me ever since. And for good reason, it would seem. By rights I should destroy you now. Less than half a year passed before you began to meddle in the affairs of the ring . . . in opposition to my most dire warnings."

"I have not interfered in the affairs of you or the ring," Odhinn replied gravely. "I have attended my own affairs as I have seen fit, and that is no concern of yours."

Jordh seemed to radiate amusement. "You have not been quite so secretive as you must have hoped. The elf-world is overrun with talking wolves, and the Children of the Wolves are spoke of with awe throughout the northlands of Midhgardh. For hatching such a secretive plot, you have managed to advertise it well."

Odhinn, chuckling to himself, walked over to a bench to sit down. Jordh was right. He had not been so secretive as he should have been. But he perceived also that, for all her righteous indignation, Jordh's threats were mostly bluff. He had seen her angry before, perhaps even frightened, that night in Hreidmar's hall when the Rhinegold had made itself known. She had come now to warn him off well ahead of time, or perhaps she was only curious. But she was not angry, and in that he saw a chance to salvage his plans.

"Jordh, you old fool, you cannot deceive me!" he said. "You are not here to threaten as much as you are having a good laugh at my expense."

"Old fool?" Jordh asked. "You are older than I, and by far the bigger fool. I would be more angry, except that your efforts have so ridiculously gone astray."

Odhinn made a gesture of hopeless denial. "What can I say? Such are the hazards of depending upon mortals."

Jordh all but laughed aloud. "'Mortals! Your wolf-clan is utterly devoted to you. The fault, old friend, is entirely your own. You should have left them to the winds of chance until you were ready for them. I am sure that is what you meant. But you love them too much. You indulge them too much. You cannot stay away from them, and you seek to shelter them from a world they cannot understand."

"I cannot deny it," Odhinn said, shaking his head sadly.

"Do not be so concerned," Jordh told him. "I find it hard to consider that a failing. In truth, I had thought that you cared nothing but for yourself and your own authority. That is what separates you from your enemies. That is also what makes them stronger. Utgardh-Loki would not care who he used, or destroyed in the process, so long as he gained from it."

Odhinn looked up at her in some surprise. "I must also admit that I had not believed that you could make the distinction. But say what you have come to say, and be done with it.''

''As you wish. It is simple enough. Stay out of Midhgardh. At least stay well away from the Volsungs. . . . No, do not look so surprised! I know the name well. In fact, I have been watching your doings for quite some time. I nearly decided to put a stop to it several years ago, when the wolflings suddenly settled within so short a distance of the dragon's lair. I could not imagine how you contrived that until I decided that you were as surprised by that as I was. Then they moved back to the south, and you encouraged it.''

''Do the Volsungs worry you?'' Odhinn asked.

''Yes, they worry me,'' Jordh admitted after a moment's hesitation. ''I got the best dragon I could contrive to be the guardian of the ring. But you have made an even better dragonslayer. I would not bother to put an end to your games, except I fear that a Volsung is perfectly capable of taking the ring from Fafnir.''

Odhinn sat for a moment, deep in thought. At last he looked up at her. ''I cannot agree to your terms. I made a promise to them, that when their children are grown and their mates grow old, they may go into the elf-world and rejoin their packs to live as wolves. That is their one great desire. If you have watched as closely as you say, then you should know that.''

Jordh considered for a moment, and Odhinn waited with subdued anticipation.

''So be it,'' she agreed at last. ''I know that I should not allow it, but it seems that I suffer the same faults as yourself. You may go at times to lead them to the elf-world. But I will tolerate no greater interference on your part.''

Odhinn leaped up, but it was too late. Having had the last word, Jordh departed in an instant, phasing back into her own realm, leaving Odhinn standing with his spear in his hand and his mouth hanging open.

But he was not greatly concerned, for in all he was pleased with the way this confrontation had turned out. He had never been greatly concerned for his own safety, but he had feared that Jordh would have destroyed his wolf-lings once his plan was discovered. He still had the Volsungs, as well as the right to visit them on occasion. That surprised him most, for Jordh's wisest decision would have been to banish them all to the elf-world. Her mistake was his gain; someday the time would come at last, and a Volsung would defeat Fafnir and win the ring.

A short distance away, a weasel threaded its sinuous way through the cover of the bushes, hopped out onto the path and became Loki. He had, of course, been aware for some time that Odhinn was up to something in the wilds of Midhgardh, and now he knew what. He knew also that the ring still existed, something he had not anticipated, and he knew where to find it. He could not go himself; Jordh had absolutely no regard for him and would destroy him in an instant. But he could arrange for an agent of his own to recover the ring for him. Or one of Odhinn's. The Volsungs would serve him as well as they served their true master. The knowledge that the ring still existed awakened memories of the short time that he had possessed the Rhinegold, and the desire for it again burned within him. He meant to have the ring.

And watching it all, unseen and unheard, was Jordh. All was going well, exactly as she had planned. Or as the prophecy of the Nornir had foretold. Radiating satisfaction, she returned to her own realm.

CHAPTER FIVE

Rerir of the Volsungs had a son, who was called Sigi, the third of the line that had descended from Volsung. Rerir and his mate Hrodney had no other. Sigi grew quickly, and he was strong and swift. Soon after, the rest of the original wolflings began to depart for the elf-world, for their mates were now coming into their later years. Rannvieg went first, for she missed Volsung and knew that he awaited her, and the others were gone before Sigi reached his twelfth year. One by one they took their true forms and slipped off into the night, while the others pretended not to look, and they were soon met in the forest by the Wanderer or the watchful Valkyrie.

The Volsungs continued to prosper, and soon their little holding was a small village. Mortal folk soon forgot their fear of the people of the Vargarbraut, and even of the forest itself, so that when Sigi was coming of age, ships began to put in at their bank, and merchants came to trade. No one regretted giving a son or daughter to a wolfling for a mate, or to take a wolfling mate, for the Children of the Wolves were considered blessed.

Eventually there came a time that young Sigi had to take a mate, and he did not have far to look. The Volsungs remembered that the Wanderer had promised that, with this generation, they were free to take mates from among their own numbers. There was one girl he had known and liked for some time, who was Kjyra of the line of Rannvieg the swift. Others of their generation had already taken mates from among their own clan, and the results had been favorable. And so when Sigi and Kjyra made their intentions known, there was no problem.

But Sigi and Kjyra had few peaceful days together. Soon there came a dark time for all the northlands, for a great horde of wild, barbaric men came out of the unknown lands of the far east. They came up north and east of the towering mountains where the world-tree stood, passing around the northern shore of the Vidvatn and dispersing into the empty lands between the Rhine and the Hronn. Whether they came intent upon raiding or settling was uncertain; they lacked the numbers to take the northlands for their own but seemed not to be aware of that. They gave no quarter and asked for none, for they knew neither mercy nor fear. But dark elves and trolls were among their numbers, so it could be guessed that the will that directed them was ultimately that of Utgardh-Loki.

Those farthest upriver fell before the threat was even known. The holding that had been Hreidmar's was taken unaware one night, and Andvari the dwarf closed the doors of his hall and did not open them again for two years. But the northmen had by far the greatest strength and they were quick to move. Within days a hundred longboats crawled upstream under straining oars to check the invasion until a counterthrust could be assembled.

The Volsungs sent two ships of their own, and they proved their skill with sword, spear and bow. Nearly every adult Volsung, male and female, went to fight the invasion. Two long years passed before they could return to their holding, and five did not come home but were freed to sit by the Allfather's seat with the guardian wolves of

Valhalla. Twice as many had taken serious injuries and departed to the elf-world to seek complete healing of their wounds. Among those who were left was Rerir, entrusting the leadership of the Volsungs to his son Sigi. And Sigi had done well during the war, both as a leader in battle and as a tracker of stealth, the greatest contest of the invasion had been won by his careful planning and quick wits. The Volsungs welcomed his leadership, and he brought them many long years of peace and contentment.

Within the first year of their return, Sigi and his mate Kjyra had the first of their children. And that proved a matter of amazement and delight for all the Volsungs, for the children of Sigi were the first twins their race had known, Sigmund and Signy by name, male and female. The following year this miracle was repeated, and again, and again, until Sigmund and Signy had nine brothers in all. And the fourth generation of the line of Volsung promised to be the heartiest of all.

Though Sigmund was less cautious and contemplative than his father, he was stronger and swifter, more given to swift and sudden action. His joy was in the hunt, not with bow or spear but in the excitement of the chase as he ran in his true form. Mortal weapons never came well to his hands. He did master the bow with deadly accuracy, but he wielded sword and spear as though they were the broom of some lordling's servant woman, aimed at trespassing cats. Still he could lead well and was highly regarded.

Signy, on the other hand, was most like her father. She was a thinker and a planner. She resembled most the mother of her line, Megelna the wolf, and was also called Gafadhur, the clever one. As she grew older, many began to wonder if it might be best that she, not her brother, should be the next leader of the Volsungs. Better yet, some thought, was that they should mate and lead their clan together, the skills of each complementing the other.

While they were twins, they were also wolflings and free to mate closer than mortal folk would wish or dare. And it seemed a likely arrangement with them as well.

They came one spring morning, two vast longboats, great sea-going warships such as seldom saw the fresh, swift waters of the Hronn. Only an experienced and capable captain, or else a very foolish one, would bring such a vessel up the inland ways, for they were as sleek and swift as falcons over the waves but too heavy and ponderous to dodge rocks and hidden banks. Now two of these hunters of the waves edged gingerly into the sandy bank at the landing of Volsung hold.

The Volsungs, of course, were hardly caught unaware. Even before the two big ships nosed in, everyone in the holding either stood ready with weapons or were with the cubs, ready for flight at a moment's notice. But that was only a precaution, for Sigi could not believe that these visitors were any immediate danger, not when they arrived in the light of day in ships that required nearly half an hour just to tie up. He counted a hundred warriors on each ship, half of what they could carry. They were matched number for number by a Volsung, wolfling or mortal, and seriously outclassed.

The lower boom of the first ship was used as a crane to lift out a long plank, but only a single warrior disembarked. Sigi gave a small signal and most of the Volsungs melted into the shadows where they remained unseen but ready. Then he stepped forward to meet the stranger, surely the leader of this party, to judge by his bearing and the richness of his dress and weapons.

"I seek Sigi, son of Rerir, Lord of the Volsungs," the stranger said in the thick accent of the northlanders. "I bear him greetings and a message from my lord."

"I am Sigi," he replied cautiously, suspecting trouble to come.

To his surprise, the foreigner, a head taller than he and as wide across the shoulders as any two Volsungs, bowed before him as though he were one of the lordlings of the lower Rhine. "My lord, I am Egil, son of Egil the Boar, trusted lieutenant of my Lord Siggier, son of Thorvald the Bear, King of Hafvang. My lord has great matters to discuss with you. I have been entrusted to speak for him in his absence and make such arrangements as we both may find fitting."

Sigi had heard of Siggier before and that did not surprise him, not after he had seen these two magnificent ships. But he did not greatly trust that name, nor any man who called himself king, not just of a holding but an entire land. And did everyone in Hafvang have fathers who were animals?

"I am Sigi, son of Rerir the Wolf," he repeated wryly, but bowed his head politely. "I extend to you the hospitality of my hall and holding and will gladly discuss matters with you in his absence."

"Thank you, my lord," Egil said, falling in step beside him as they started for the main hall.

"And what are these matters to be discussed, if I may ask?" Sigi inquired.

"My lord seeks a bride, a very special bride," Egil explained candidly. "It is his hope that the Volsungs may find him a worthy mate."

"Oh? Surely he does not want to marry me!" Sigi exclaimed in jest.

Egil laughed. "Close, but not quite. He seeks the hand of your daughter Signy."

Thorvald, son of Hjalmer, had been a mountainous man, tall and powerful, quick to laugh and to anger, and wiser and quicker of thought than his slow speech and simple manners suggested. In his day he had been called Redbeard as well, for his own, forked and braided, was always tucked into his belt, and he swung a double-headed ax as though it were the hammer Mjollnir. Thorvald had been good and benevolent when he willed it, but he had also his darker side. He had inherited young a holding that had been among the largest and richest in the northlands, and in the years that followed, it grew many times. He was never openly ambitious, attacking his neighbors without cause. But any cause, even the smallest provocation, was enough to earn his fullest wrath.

But Thorvald had one neighbor he could not take in battle, and he never tried. To the north lay a holding fully as large as his own. Lady Asa ruled there, and she was Thorvald's match in both cunning and ambition. Perhaps they recognized this from the start, for the hostilities that could have grown quickly between them turned instead to an alliance.

Thorvald and Asa had one child, a son by the name Siggier. In appearance he was like his father, tall and powerfully built as were most men of the northlands. In thought he was more like his mother; deep, brooding and utterly selfish. When Thorvald had died suddenly five years earlier, Lady Asa, still fairly young, and her son had fought for control of his holding, for both would have all or nothing. Asa had the advantage of experience and a strong following, and her claim was beyond dispute. But Siggier, it was seen, had the greater ambition. For Asa had died suddenly and very mysteriously, and he had seized all.

Siggier was a man that few could trust. Lords of even the smallest holdings, who perhaps did not even know who lived two valleys away, knew and feared his name. Siggier was an outwardly honest king, and his numerous wars

were always cloaked in justice. But there were also new
pirates who prowled the seas and raided the rivers, and the
few survivors they left spoke of ships so large that there
could be no doubt who their master was.

Nor did Sigi trust this man, and for good reason. Siggier
alone had the strength of arms to pin the wolflings within
their holding and overwhelm them. The Hafvang lord
could land twenty or more of his great ships down river,
each one bearing as many as two hundred warriors, and
take the Volsungs by surprise. Moreover, Sigi thought this
was a man arrogant enough to ignore the warning of the
Valkyrie that the Volsungs were a favored and protected
race, the chosen of the Allfather. He was loath to agree to
this deal, and for the same reason that he dared not refuse.

But Egil spoke fairly, explaining that Siggier desired a
Volsung bride not for any special honor, but so that he
might have a Volsung son, the very best son he could find
to rule fairly when he was gone. And so it was that Signy,
overriding her father's wishes, struck her own bargain, for
she too feared this lordling's wrath and hoped to protect
her clan by giving him what he wanted. But she insisted
upon this in return, that she would be free to return to her
own clan when Siggier had his heir. And so Egil went
away soon with this message, and that Siggier could claim
his bride as soon as it pleased him.

The ships came again on a bright morning in late spring,
laboring up the river under the rhythmic sweep of broad
oars. Sunlight glinted on the bright trim and brilliant colors
of the ornamental shields that hung along their siderails
and from the shining helmets and breastplates of the warriors who drew the oars. One by one the immense warships nosed gently onto shore, moving with deceptive ease
for their size and the strength of the current where they
dared to pull onto the sandy bank.

A long plank was lifted ashore and Siggier of Hafvang stepped out. He was in small ways like his father, for he was taller even than most of his own men, tall and powerful enough, with such a reach of sword, that he could likely hold the advantage over a Volsung in a contest of sword or spear. But his hair and short beard were not his father's rich red but black. He was easily counted as handsome, even majestic in his appearance, but he possessed few of the qualities that the wolflings admired, and his calm self-assurance was almost repulsive to them. Many of the Volsungs, looking upon him for the first time, were disappointed and pitied Signy for her fate. But she had been wiser than that and had known what to expect.

And so it was that Siggier of Hafvang and Signy of the Wolves were wed in a forest clearing, according to the manner of the Volsungs since their earliest day, and the Allfather's name was invoked to bless their union. All the Volsung clan stood gathered about the edges of the clearing, while the bright warriors of Hafvang marched at attention in ordered files of honor. But Sigmund was saddened by the loss of his sister, whom he loved above all else. And in his heart he was deeply troubled, so that he would not look up as the new couple turned and walked past.

That night there was a celebration in the forest holding of the Volsungs, a feast in the honor of the wedding of Signy and Siggier. It was, perhaps, not much of a celebration as far as Siggier's men were concerned, for they had brought little to drink with them and then found, to their surprise and consternation, that the Volsungs did not drink ale, mead or even wine. The food, however, did make up somewhat for that loss. There was venison from the woods and salmon from the stream, cooked with last season's nuts and the first spring fruit, as well as the best cheese.

In honor of the customs of their guests, Signy did not enter until all were seated. When all was ready, Sigmund discreetly withdrew from the main hall and circled around to the front. Even though it was full night, the holding was illuminated in yellow lamplight, and the sounds of merry-making filled the air. Sigmund joined Signy just outside the door, and they paused for a moment to watch.

"I wish that we might join them," he said. "I know that I would enjoy that more."

"Why?" Signy asked. "What do they have that will not be at our table?"

"Happiness, perhaps," Sigmund replied and turned to her. "Perhaps I do not want you to go."

"Perhaps I do not want to go. The world will not end just because our lives are changed."

"No, the world will not end. But too much will no longer be the same. The leaves will not be as green, nor the forest as deep and welcoming. Spring will not seem as full and alive. Winter nights will not seem as close and comfortable without you to sit beside me at the fire."

Signy smiled. "Foolish dreamer! You have listened too often to the plans that others have made for us."

Sigmund shrugged, turning away. "It seems like a good idea to me."

Signy came up beside him and took his hand. "Our lives are long, so grant me just twenty years more. Then, on one clear spring night, we will meet again in the deep forests of the elf-world and make of our lives only what we wish. For now I have a greater responsibility, an obligation to the Volsungs and to the Allfather that I must fulfill before I can be free."

"Until then," Sigmund agreed and went with her into the hall.

The festivities began in earnest but were only minutes old when a sudden tenseness in the air filled the crowded

hall. Siggier stirred abruptly and sat up straight, a movement so quick that those about him looked toward the far
end of the room to see what had startled him. In the
shadows of the far wall stood what appeared to be an old
man, wrapped in a long cloak and wearing a broad-brimmed
hat, one side pulled down but failing to hide the fact that
the stranger wore a patch over one eye. He had come
unheard and unseen, to stand leaning on his spear as he
watched the gathering.

"Who is that old man?" Siggier demanded. Sigi was
surprised, for the two glared at one another like old and
mortal enemies.

"That is the Wanderer, a servant of the Allfather," he
replied. "He taught and guided the first wolflings, although he seldom comes among us now."

Sigi rose to face the Wanderer and bowed his head
politely. "My lord, this is indeed a pleasant surprise.
Come take my seat, and join us at our celebration."

The Volsung was more sincere in his welcome than in
any of the fine words he had been forced to use that day,
a fact that Siggier noted with veiled displeasure. The
Wanderer approached slowly. Everyone in the hall was
silent, watching him with curiosity and apprehension.

"Your offer is kind, but I cannot stay," he said. "I
come only to deliver a present, a gift from the Allfather
himself."

"A wedding present?" Sigi asked.

"Alas, no. I cannot say who it is for, but it will come
only to the hand of the one it was made and intended for.
Come with me outside and we will put it to the test."

He did not even pause to see if they would follow but
turned and walked purposefully out of the hall. The guests
looked at one another in surprise, then rose and followed
quickly, fearful that the Wanderer might in his obvious
haste bestow his gift before they could arrive. Confused

Volsungs and Northlanders approached from every direction, but the Wanderer seemed not to notice. He marched up to the largest tree in the center of the holding, a massive oak.

He waited, looking up at the tree as he leaned upon his spear, until everyone in the holding had gathered about. At last he drew himself up and handed his spear to the hesitant Lord of the Volsungs, then reached into the folds of his cloak to draw forth a sword. He held it up at arm's length, point skyward, and the metal glowed with a fierce white radiance while sheets of flame flowed across its surface. Then he stepped forward and rammed the blade into the trunk of the tree. It slid in up to its hilt so easily that a hole might have opened in the wood to receive it.

"Behold the sword Gram!" he declared, reaching for his spear. "The gift of Odhinn. It was made by Heimdall of special metals and given a measure of power that dwells in the Allfather's spear. No hand may draw it from the wood save the one it was intended for. He who may draw it should hold it with care, for it was made to serve him in his need, and he should let no one touch it, unless he should pass it to his son on the day he departs from this realm."

"Then it was meant for a Volsung?" Siggier asked, suddenly eager.

"I did not say that," the Wanderer replied, turning to him. "There is more than one way to depart from this realm, as all men do in time."

"Then how do we know who should have it?"

The Wanderer indicated the sword. "Try to draw it forth. If it comes to you, then it is yours."

Siggier hesitated. In truth he was fearful of trying, for if he failed, it would not reflect well on either himself or his strength. But for the same reason he could not refuse. He stepped forward and placed both hands upon the hilt of the sword and pulled with all his strength. When that failed he placed one and then both boots against the trunk of the tree and pulled even harder. After a time he was forced to relent; the hilt was still set tight against the trunk of the tree.

"This is magic!" he spat angrily. "Few men can boast of greater strength than I possess, but I cannot draw that sword."

"Of course it is magic," the Wanderer replied. "This is not a contest of strength; the sword will come only to the one who needs it most. Be comforted by that, for perhaps you will never have such need."

Signy stirred suddenly, and she was pale and shaken. "Sigmund, I fear that the sword is meant for you."

All were silent, for she had spoken louder than she had meant. But Sigmund only laughed. "Then I shall be the last to try it. Then no one will be able to say that I drew it by some accident."

Therefore, they did as he said. Everyone gathered in a long line, both Siggier's warriors and all the Volsungs, male and female. The last to try was Signy herself, and yet the sword remained firmly embedded in the tree. She stepped back and indicated for her brother to try.

"Your sword, Sigmund," she said.

He stepped forward no less hesitantly than Siggier had. The sword was no pleasant gift for the threat of danger that accompanied it. The sword seemed almost to leap into the hand that he laid upon it, as if he drew it from its sheath. He held it aloft, flinching, as flames played across its blade. After a moment the flames vanished and the glow died away, and he held it down to look at it fearfully.

"You may safely touch the blade," the Wanderer said. "The magic in it is at your service, and by no means will it harm you."

"But . . . how do I make it work for me?" Sigmund

asked, touching the blade. It seemed to be made of silver but was harder than dwarf-made steel.

"Use it as you would any sword. The magic will enhance your strength and skill. The blade will never dull or break. Lay it against metal or stone and will its power to life, and it will cut with great heat."

"Why did you not just give it to him in the first place?" Siggier demanded sourly.

The Wanderer turned to him with a look of patient tolerance. "The sword had to go to him of its own accord, so that his claim upon it would be complete . . . and so that no one will think to dispute that claim. He is protected against its powers, but it will as quickly fry the hands off some foolish thief."

"But who are you?" Siggier demanded. "What do you possess?"

The Wanderer, who had turned to leave, paused and looked back at him. "My name is my own, but if you sense a deception, then surely you can guess. And my powers are beyond any strength that you might hope to possess."

With that he turned and walked away through the crowd, disappearing into the night.

CHAPTER SIX

The years that followed passed with almost brooding slowness, but with the coming of each spring, another year was counted, and the Volsungs were less ill at ease. Sigi remained as the leader of the Volsungs, even though it was time that Sigmund should have assumed that duty, but no one had to question his reasons. Sigi attended to the general problems of the holding while Sigmund addressed his talents to special tasks, an arrangement that worked well. Soon after Signy's departure, Sigmund began to lead small groups by ship to Vikfjallaland, where they secretly restored and expanded the old mountain holding of the Volsungs and laid in equipment and supplies so that, should they be forced to withdraw there, such things as they needed would be waiting for them. Sigi also ordered the construction of two new ships.

A messenger came from Siggier once or twice a year, and he always assured the Volsungs that all was well and that Signy was happy. Indeed she did seem to have tamed Siggier somewhat, for he made no more conquests upon his neighbors, and the great pirate ships that had roamed the waves suddenly disappeared. The Volsungs did not know just how Signy fared, for the messenger spoke of contentment and peace in such glowing terms that they

could believe little of what he said. Only one report they
did not doubt, for Siggier had the son he desired. Signy
had her first child, Geir, barely a year after her departure,
and Thrain came only two years later. But even that was
not good news, for they could guess by what the messenger
said—and did not say—that the children had been born in
mortal form. Obviously they were indeed mortal; the
Allfather's blessing had not been extended for the first
time in the history of their race. Their one hope was that
Siggier preferred matters this way, mortal children with
certain immortal traits, but not wolflings themselves.

Nine long years passed in this way, as the Volsungs
waited and yet Siggier made no move against them. Then,
in the spring of the next year, the messenger came yet
again, this time with a request. He reported that Signy was
lonely for her father and her twin, and asked that they
should come, with Siggier's kindest invitations, to Hafvang
to spend some time with her that spring. Sigi hardly knew
how to reply, so at last he sent the messenger away with
the promise that he would come as soon as he might.

As soon as the messenger was gone, Sigi called about
him those whose advice he trusted most. Signy, of course,
was gone, and Kjyra, Sigi's own mate, had gone ahead
into the elf-world a year before. Sigmund had long since
taken a mate, Sigrune, so named because she was as quick
and fearless as the Captain of the Valkyries. Most of
Sigmund's brothers were now grown, but none had any
pretentions of being leaders and were content to follow the
commands of their father and eldest brother.

"How can he presume that we will walk so blindly into
his trap?" Sigmund demanded indignantly as their meeting
commenced at the table in the main hall.

"Siggier may be sincere," Kari of the youngest twins
said. "He is far less violent than in the past. And I cannot

believe that he would invite an open battle into his own hall.''

"It is a trap," Sigmund insisted. "Signy would never ask that we come to her. Even if it was safe, she still would not ask because she would know that we cannot be certain.''

"Perhaps I am missing something," Kaldan, another of the brothers, said. "Violent though Siggier was and may yet be, he was always a practical pirate. What does he stand to gain?''

"The sword," Sigmund replied simply. "He has wanted it from the moment he first saw it. He wants it so badly that he has waited this long, being this careful, in laying his trap.''

"Can the power of the sword protect us?" Sigi asked.

Sigmund did not respond at once. Instead he drew the blade, hung in its sheath at his belt, and held it up. The blade flashed radiantly as he drew it forth, but only for an instant before it was still. He laid it on the table, then looked up at his father.

"That, I fear, is about the limit of its powers. It will not throw bolts of lightning or sheets of flame. It will not melt iron or stone at the touch as the Wanderer said it would. It does not even increase my skill with the weapon, although I have not yet had a chance to test it in actual battle.''

"Then it does not have such powers?" Sigi asked.

Sigmund shrugged. "I do not doubt that it has every power described by the Wanderer and more besides. But in the nine years that I have held it, none of those powers have responded to me.''

He paused a moment and sighed heavily. "I see only one sure answer. I will break the sword and take the pieces so that Siggier might see them, and tell him that the sword failed me. Then he will see that his prize really was not worth having. I would give it to him whole, if I was more certain that it would answer him no better.''

Sigi, ill at ease, shook his head slowly. ''I do not like the thought that we should destroy the Allfather's gift.''

''The Allfather's gift has brought us greater danger than it was meant to eliminate,'' Sigmund replied. ''Now, in its destruction, it can serve us as it was meant. I will take it well away from here, in case there is some danger in releasing its magic. Should the Wanderer try to stop me, then he can take back his weapon intact. For the trouble it has brought, I mean to either destroy it or be rid of it.''

Sigmund crossed the river in a rowboat and made his way toward that part of the Vargarbraut the wolflings called Forest Hall, where the first Children of the Wolves had once lived. Much of the great forest was hilly and rolling, although less so than along portions of the Rhine farther to the south. But the only place within the boundaries of the woods where large, exposed blocks of solid stone were to be found was in the area about Forest Hall.

Sigmund searched the area of Forest Hall carefully, looking for what he considered to be exactly the right stone. In truth he was delaying as long as possible, not for lack of resolve but because he considered it best that the Wanderer should come back and reclaim the sword. But after half an hour of such procrastination, he decided that he would have to go ahead with his plan.

Evening was falling by the time he selected his stone. The sun was already behind the hills, and the forest paths were growing dark. The boulder sat off to one side of the main path, taller than himself and wider still, and six long strides in length. Sigmund looked it over and drew his sword swiftly, lifting it high over his head. The blade seemed to flash brighter than it had when he had first drawn it from the tree, perhaps in alarmed protest of what he was about to do. Then he brought it down, edge first, with all his strength against the upper edge of the boulder.

Sparks and splinters of stone flew as the blade hit, and Sigmund was forced to close his eyes momentarily against both. When he looked again, he was not surprised to find the blade intact, although buried twice its length in the stone. What did surprise him was that a wide crack continued to spread slowly away from the cut, creaking and snapping loudly as it moved over the top of the boulder and down the front. After a long moment the cracks met somewhere near the back of the stone, and the sides of the block, neatly halved, fell away with a crash to either side.

Sigmund looked at the sword in disgust. "Why, after nine years, do you have to start that now? Do you not suppose it to be a little late?"

"It certainly is," a voice behind him said. He spun quickly, startled at the sound of a voice that he had not heard in years but would never forget. Siggier stood a short distance behind him, dressed in full armor for battle, but the weapon that he held in his hand was a wizard's short wand. That wand was aimed at him, and the northlander spoke words that even Sigmund's sharp ears could not catch. The next moment faded into darkness.

The darkness began to recede in what seemed like only a moment later, although Sigmund knew that at least one day had passed. It had been early evening; now the sun was shining with the warmth and brightness of full day. He felt as if he had not actually been unconscious, but merely lifted out of time one moment and returned much later. He saw that he was lying in a small shelter against the solid bulwark in the very stern of one of the immense warships. The middle part of the longboat was filled almost to overflowing with scores of warriors, now busy about various tasks as they sat among boxes and sacks of supplies, or loot.

The helmsman stood directly across from where Sigmund lay, both hands on the tiller as he stared ahead. A crossbar connected the two fixed rudders, and there was also a retractable centerboard now bolted into place. This was clearly a ship of advanced design, advances that even Siggier's people had not known only nine years before. Sigmund tried to sit up, hampered as he was by heavy chains on his wrists. The manacles were made of some strange gray metal, very soft but too thick for him to bend or break, oily in appearance but dry to the touch. These in turn were attached to a length of chain of suspiciously high quality, short enough that, had he jumped overboard, the chain would have held him high enough above the waves to keep him alive until he could be fetched back.

"So, you rejoin us at last."

Sigmund looked up, startled. Siggier had obviously been seated on the rail on the other side of a wooden box that formed a wall of his shelter.

"You do not seem particularly surprised to see me," Siggier said as he looked down at the helpless Volsung, his tone even more subtly cruel because of its polite veneer. "You actually came out from under the sleeping spell much sooner than any mortal. I see that you are admiring my ship. I have new allies. Powerful allies, and they have taught me many things. My new ships have centerboards and rudders, such as the Wanderer has taught your people to use. I have other things, other weapons, such as you have never dreamed."

He paused for a moment to bring out a slender wooden wand. It was soft and very flexible wood, certainly no weapon or anything more dangerous than a good switch. He touched it lightly to Sigmund, who abruptly shifted into his true form and stayed that way no matter how hard he tried to make the transformation back. Then the wand was withdrawn, and he returned to human form.

Siggier smiled. "A gift from my friend. A peeled stem of mistletoe from the elf-world, which has the power to break all spells. Consider also the manacles on your wrists. That metal possesses a similar quality, resistant to spells of cutting and breaking. You might have also noticed, when you were in wolf form, that you could no more extract your paws than you can now remove your hands."

"Your friend is very generous," Sigmund observed. "What does he expect in return?"

"Just my friendship, and the assurance that I will further his cause in advancing my own. And now that I have the sword of the Aesir as well, I might soon be able to dictate a few of my own terms. At the least I can sell it at a very high price indeed, but I plan to keep it. Once I can command its powers, I will also be able to command more respect from my associate."

"So your friend has now become an associate," Sigmund observed. "Your friend seems to be somewhat less than friendly, or at least less than trustworthy."

Siggier frowned, distracted from the line of pleasant thoughts he had been following. "Friendship and trust are of no concern. Your father tried to make a deal with me; he gave me what I asked and hoped that I would be satisfied. He might have used his advantage to be rid of me, but he did not. I created my own advantage, as long as it took, and now I have exactly what I want. Now I have no delusions about my actual worth to my associate. I cannot defeat him, so I make myself impossible to dispose of. The sword will insure that."

Siggier paused for a moment, watching his prisoner closely. "You simply cannot understand that, can you? I do not question your intelligence; your sister is surely the brightest person I have ever met. She thought she knew exactly how to lead me about and control my every move, but for all her wisdom and cleverness she simply lacks the

deviousness and cunning to see below the surface. You
look at life through the eyes of a wolf, and everything
seems so simple to you.

"But I see that I am only bewildering you. A poor
choice of words, that last; life, from your perspective,
undoubtedly seems quite complicated. It makes revenge a
pointless gesture. But I still want you to live long enough
to appreciate the completeness of my victory. And I do
want your sister to see the wreck of her own great plans."

With that he rose and walked away, leaving Sigmund to
his thoughts. And he did have much to think about. He
could guess easily enough just who Siggier's fine friend
must be. That was a matter for the Wanderer and the
Valkyries, if they did not already know. What did concern
Sigmund greatly was the fate of the Volsungs. He hoped
that Siggier had been satisfied with the sword and his
single prisoner, but he doubted that. They must have been
taken by surprise; they had been so concerned with Siggier's
trap that they had, for the very first time, failed to consider
that the trap could be brought to them. Siggier said nothing
on the subject, which led Sigmund to hope that his victory
had been far less complete than he had wished.

These thoughts occupied his mind for the next two days
as the great warships made their way up the coast to
Hafvang, turning at last into a deep bay. The ships did not
even try to push ashore but slipped easily between long
piers that extended out into the bay. Sigmund was ignored
for a time in the rush to tie up and unload, but tall warriors
eventually did come for him. They took him from the ship,
skirting the edges of the largest holding that Sigmund had
ever seen, and into the forest to the north.

After a few minutes they came to a small clearing, and
Sigmund now began to understand the nature of Siggier's
revenge. Eleven stocks had been built, side by side in a
long row, and the first nine were occupied by each of his

nine younger brothers. The guards forced him into the tenth, not removing his manacles until he was safely locked in. The eleventh place to his right remained empty; he first suspected that it was meant for his sister. But when the guards never returned he realized that it must have been built for his father, who had not been among the captives.

"So, you did make it after all," Kari said after the warriors had departed. "We were given to wonder what had become of you. We knew that you had gone into the forest, and we hoped that Siggier had missed you."

"No, he made certain of me first, since he wanted the sword more than anything," Sigmund replied. "He was crafty enough to know what I would do after his messenger left, and he was waiting for me."

"That can hardly be helped," Halvard said. "We can only hope now that Siggier will find it impossible to control the sword. Surely the great ones who made it will not allow it to remain in such hands."

"That I cannot say. Perhaps the Wanderer will come soon enough, or perhaps the Valkyries, and Siggier will see the flaw in his plans. I doubt that his new friend will be able—or even willing—to protect him."

"His friend?" Kari asked. "Then he does have new allies?"

"Allies?" Sigmund laughed grimly. "I would say that he has given himself up to a new master. His friends might be able to challenge the authority of the Allfather on their own ground, but not in this realm. But what of the holding? How were you captured? Siggier made a point of telling me nothing."

"Magic of some type," Kari explained. "And very selective, for it found only us. The attack came about two hours after you left. Father went to do what he could to get everyone out of the holding, while we went to try to distract the attackers. I guess that we were successful in that.''

"Then most escaped?'' Sigmund asked.

"I suppose so; I did not see much of it. They began throwing large bags of flaming liquid through the air with their launch-arm machines. . . .''

"Catapults,'' Sorli suggested. "Our ship was packed with them, and the sailors called them catapults.''

"Catapults,'' Kari agreed. "This might have worked, except that they shot well over their target for so long. I believe that nearly everyone was out of the holding by the time they found their range. The noise of the things going over alerted us. But I do remember seeing more than one wolf running with his coat in flames. Sigrune . . . Sigrune was all but knocked over by one of the things. At least she only ran a few moments before she fell.''

Sigmund did not reply, but sat for a moment in silence. He accepted the death of his mate as his nature allowed, as something he would have to mourn when time permitted, if he himself survived. He had been prepared for many possibilities. After only a short pause he looked up. "But you think that father led most of the wolves to safety?''

"He must have,'' Kari replied. "I guess that he got away with two-thirds or more of the wolflings. Of course, none of the mortal folk escaped alive. Many were captured as thralls but were later ordered slain, or so we heard.''

"At least there is some satisfaction in knowing that Siggier's plans failed him,'' Sigmund said, mostly to himself.

"Failed?'' Valgard asked in disbelief.

"Yes, I would say that. Had everything gone as he wished, as it might well have, then we would be the only wolflings alive now. Do you think that they went north to the old holding in Vikfjallaland?''

"How?'' Kari asked. "Siggier has our ships, and they

cannot cross the sea north of Hafvang without boats. They are either hiding in the forest, or they retreated into the elf-world. I hope that the latter is the case.''

"So be it. . . ,'' Sigmund began, but paused when he felt the magical sleep overpower him again. The last thing he saw was a large gray wolf stepping cautiously out of the deeper shadows of the forest. His first thought was that the Volsungs had come to rescue their captive members, but he quickly saw his mistake. Volsungs were larger than true wolves, but this beast was far larger still, easily as large as a pony. Now, at last, he had no doubts about the identity of Siggier's new friend.

CHAPTER SEVEN

Siggier marched purposefully up the hill to his big, new hall, only just completed, with his six most trusted warriors, his personal bodyguard, following almost in his steps. His plans had gone well, if not as well as he had hoped. His new spies, gifts from his friend, continued to report that the surviving Volsungs were still running in their animal forms, moving east and slightly north into wild and mostly unsettled areas. Their course did not stray or wander, and they traveled with such speed and determination that he knew they must have some destination in mind. He meant to mark the location of the world-gate well as a pathway of future raids. In a day or two the world would be free of all Volsungs, except for those few that were safely under his control, the last major obstacle to his conquests.

The only remaining task at hand was for him to learn, either from Signy or her twin, the true nature of the great task that they were to perform. He thought that there was some great object that they were to recover, and if Odhinn would go to such lengths to have it, then it must be precious indeed. He entered the hall by the main door and made his way through the main room where tables were hastily being erected for a victory feast that night. He

continued without pausing, following the passage that led
to his own apartment in the southwest corner overlooking
the bay. Signy's room was adjacent to his own but not
adjoining; he had decided years before that he did not want
that cunning, half-wild creature in his own bed except
when he felt up to dealing with her.

He knocked heavily on the door and entered without
awaiting her answer. Signy stood beside the bed looking
up at him with an expression that he could not read,
surprise perhaps, or just patience, and he paused a moment
to regard her. Even in human dress she still looked alien,
elvish in size and build, but more than half animal in
appearance. Her tumbled shock of hair was brindled gray,
the color of her mane in her true form. Immense black
eyes peered out from beneath, glittering with intelligence
but far from human. In appearance she was at once both
delicate and dangerous; even he had never tamed her and,
therefore, did not trust her.

"I am back," he began hesitantly, no longer certain of
what he wanted to say.

Signy nodded once. "Welcome back, my lord."

"I have come to explain matters to you," he continued
as he stepped farther into the room. "These past few years
we have been playing a curious game, although you did
not recognize it as such. The game is now over. I have
allied myself with Utgardh-Loki, and he has given me a
great deal of magic that will make my armies invincible. I
have ships now such as the world has never seen and a
great many new and deadly weapons. I have spies, landvaetir
such as can move swiftly and unseen. And now I have the
Allfather's magic sword."

"The wolflings?" Signy asked, suddenly recognizing
the sword that hung at his belt.

"The Volsungs are destroyed. Your father is dead, and
your brothers are my captives. I have them in stocks in the

forest north of here, where one of them will die each night. Your twin Sigmund I shall save for last.''

For a moment Signy only stared at him, but as her alarm passed she seemed to draw in like an animal about to spring. Her face remained expressionless, but her eyes flashed with fire. The guards, needing no instructions, lifted their loaded crossbows. Signy glanced about and, after a moment's consideration, straightened to stand calm and erect.

''That is better,'' Siggier said approvingly. ''Now, I certainly do not want anything to happen to you, so I am going to assign you a permanent bodyguard. At least two warriors will be with you at all times, so if you ever want to bathe, then you had better do it in your fur. And I do not think that you should go outside at all in the next ten days.''

He turned, and the guards filed out the door before him. He paused at the doorway and looked back a final time. ''We will have a celebration tonight . . . to celebrate the extinction of your race. I want you to be there as a guest of honor.''

The gathering in Siggier's great hall that night was a quiet, almost stately one. His warriors, who preferred to celebrate their victories with wine and song and noisy pranks, had retired to the village to seek parties of their own. This feast was for his captains and lieutenants, and especially for the rich merchants who had turned his holding into the largest town in the known world. Siggier spoke not only of his defeat of the Volsungs, but also of his alliance with Utgardh-Loki and his many plans for the future. A number of his guests were alarmed to discover this, although no one spoke against him. In truth his captains and many of his most powerful merchants had known this for some time, so he was in no danger of losing his most important supporters.

Signy sat beside him, deep in thought. He did not doubt that she was plotting dire vengeance, but did not care so long as it kept her quiet. He knew that she would not be with him much longer, probably not more than a few weeks. One day she would slip away from her guards, and in an instant she would be gone, or perhaps he would arrange some accident and let her go. He had hated her brother for receiving the sword, and he hated all Volsungs for being what he was not. But his hate was quickly fading now that he bore the sword, and the Volsungs would soon be gone from his world. Siggier was very pleased with himself that night and felt that he could afford to be generous.

That mood was to pass quickly later that evening. Siggier was surprised when he saw Signy start and even begin to rise, then settle back into her chair with a look of relief and satisfaction. Following her gaze, he saw that same cloaked figure that had interrupted his wedding feast years before. The Wanderer stood leaning on his spear not ten paces away, looking over the northlander with an aloof, appraising manner that most men would find irritating and that Siggier found intolerable. He was even more irritated to know that his discomfort was plain.

"If you think that you have come to set all of your plans straight, then you had best consider again," Siggier said hotly, then began to restore his calm. "Of course, if that was the case, then I suppose that I would have been visited by the Valkyries rather than your own worthy self."

"No, I do not plan violence," the Wanderer said. "I have no need. Once I set matters into motion, they will carry themselves to my desired end whatever you might do to stop it."

"New plans?" Siggier asked. "Your plans seem to have failed you on more than one occasion already. I have the sword, and the Volsungs are destroyed."

"The Volsungs, for the most part, are very much alive and will be departing from this realm in the morning," the Wanderer said sharply. "I do not care how far you spread your lies. But you are a fool if you tell them to me, and a greater fool if you repeat them to yourself. Nor is the sword of any use to you."

"But the sword remains in my possession," Siggier pointed out. "I have a certain friend who would pay dearly to possess it. I also hold the lives of the two remaining Volsungs, along with nine . . . eight of their brothers. I suspect that the reason you did not descend upon me with fire and lightning is because you want these items back, the sword and the two Volsungs."

"As you realized from the start, or you would not have dared this attack." The Wanderer sounded somewhat subdued, and even Signy noted that incautious remark as being too revealing.

Siggier sat back and smiled. "I suggest that we work out a trade, whereby we each get what we want most. Which is of greatest importance to you, the sword or the Volsungs?"

"I could have a hundred such swords made tomorrow," the Wanderer admitted cautiously. "I could even have more Volsungs made, if needed, but there is an element of time involved."

Siggier leaned forward, feeling himself in firm control of the situation. "Let us speak plainly. You need these two Volsungs. I, on the other hand, need to be able to control this sword. Need I speak more plainly? You show me how to command this sword, and I will give you the two Volsungs."

The Wanderer considered that, and nodded slowly. "Very well. You recall, do you not, how command of the sword was transferred to Sigmund? We must repeat that process."

The Wanderer did not have far to look. Siggier's new

home was so large that a living oak of some size was
enclosed within the main hall, its branches now hung with
lamps. Large panes of glass, a gift from Utgardh-Loki,
were set into the roof to give it light, protected from the
elements by wooden shutters that could be drawn back.
The Wanderer stepped up to the tree and Siggier, in his
eagerness, was right beside him.

"Draw the sword and ram it point-first into the tree,"
the Wanderer instructed. "You will find that very little
effort is needed to drive it all the way up to its hilt. The
one who draws it forth again will be able to command it."

Siggier quickly drew the sword. It responded for the
first time since he had taken it, flashing once as it left its
sheath, then bursting forth in a blaze of brilliant light.
Siggier found that actually holding an object glowing with
raw power was a far more unsettling experience than he
had anticipated. Gathering his resolve, he rammed the
point into the thick bark of the tree. As the Wanderer had
said, it slid all the way up to its hilt as easily as if a hole
of precise dimensions had been waiting to receive it.

Siggier paused a moment, staring at the embedded sword,
then put both hands on its handle and gave it a swift jerk,
expecting that it would come out as easily as it had gone
in. The only result was that he nearly pulled himself hard
against the trunk of the tree. One more experimental tug
informed him that the sword would not come out at his
touch, and the implications quickly followed. He turned to
the Wanderer, still too startled to be enraged, but the
mysterious figure only held him in icy regard as it thinned
and vanished. Then Siggier realized the full extent of how
he had been tricked.

Odhinn hurried back to the world-gate as quickly as
Sleipnir could carry him, and not so much because he was
afraid of Jordh's discovering him. He wanted free of this

realm, where all his hopes and plans seemed destined to go awry. The great hall of Valhalla was dark and empty, the only light coming from the massive fireplaces at either end. The warrior guardians were gone to their rest; only Geri and Freki were there to meet him at the door. But he was not surprised to find Brynhild awaiting him inside, for he knew why she was there.

"I have just returned from Midhgardh," she said as he entered, obviously piqued. "I brought back with me the spirit of Valgard, son of Sigi, slain by a wolf of Jotunheim as he sat with his head in the stocks outside Siggier's hall. Needless to say, the wolf had to bite his head and hands off to get him out of the stocks."

"I know," Odhinn said wearily as he pushed past her. "I was just there."

"Then what did you do?" Brynhild demanded as she fell in beside him. "Did you free them?"

"No, I could not. I did not dare. Not directly."

Brynhild was so surprised that for a moment she simply stood and stared, then hurried to catch up with him. "What do you mean, you could not? What can Siggier do to prevent it?"

Odhinn sighed heavily as he sank to the nearest bench. Brynhild had just become important to his plans, and so he saw no hope but to tell her everything she needed to know to help him best. He began by reminding her of the incident of the Rhinegold, now over a hundred years past, and her own part in that. He told her of the forging of the ring, of its hiding in Fafnir's den, and of Jordh's prophecies of what their future held. He spoke to her then of his own plans, and the part that the Volsungs were meant to serve.

"My plans are so near to failure that I have decided to try a very desperate measure," he concluded. "Sigi gave me the idea by taking the Volsungs toward the world-gate into Alfheim, although I cannot guess how he learned of its location. I have let them find their gate, and in the morning I will open it for them to go through. And, if I am very fortunate indeed, Jordh will think that all the Volsungs have left her realm, and she will relax her watch on Fafnir and the ring.

"Do you not begin to see? I cannot free Sigmund or Signy myself, nor allow any of my servants such as yourself to use their powers to do so. Sigmund and Signy must free themselves, although you and I can unobtrusively steer matters to their advantage. If all the younger sons of Sigi must die to accomplish this, then so be it. You will bring me their spirits, and they will be restored to life, then sent on into the elf-world."

"A very chancy plan indeed," Brynhild remarked.

"We can arrange circumstances that should allow Signy to free her brother, if she is as wise and clever as I believe. Already I have removed the sword of power from Siggier's possession, so that Sigmund will find it waiting for him."

"But why do you need Signy as well as Sigmund?" Brynhild asked.

"Because she is as capable as her brother of slaying the dragon. What she may lack in strength, she more than makes up in cunning. And Sigmund will be more willing to complete his task if Signy is with him. And also because, if need be, they can keep their race alive through one more generation. They will flee northward to the secret holding that Volsung founded a hundred years ago, and which Sigmund has already restored. That will put them within a hundred miles of Fafnir."

Siggier might have killed all his prisoners that first night, out of revenge for having lost the sword. He considered it very seriously for quite some time. However, he never acted rashly but considered his options from every angle, and so he did not. He realized that not just the recovery of the sword depended upon keeping both Sigmund and Signy alive; they were his insurance against the wrath of the Aesir. But he decided to permit the nine younger brothers to die one each night, according to his original plan. That would serve to pressure the Wanderer into returning to negotiate for their release.

The sons of Sigi spent the night in magical sleep, unaware of the events that involved them. When the Volsungs awoke the next morning, they found a great many questions and few answers. They woke at about the same time, since the first to stir had little trouble rousing the others. Sigmund's first awareness was of Kari, seated beside him, swearing and cursing like a northland pirate. Sigmund soon found ample cause for his youngest brother's pique. His neck was cramped from a night of hanging limply through the hole of the stocks, and his back felt little better. Being wet with a heavy morning's dew only made matters worse.

"Will you kindly restrain your complaints?" he asked Kari politely. "I am surprised to find that I do not have a headache. But I shall surely have one in very short order if you do not shut up."

"Oh, I am ever so sorry," Kari answered. "Indeed, I do seem to be giving myself one as well. Nor would I dream of complaining to our good host, although these are decidedly not the best beds in the house. What say we ring up a servant and inquire about breakfast?"

Then Kari reflected a moment as matters caught up with him, and he looked up. "Now why would Siggier put us back under that sleeping spell?"

"Valgard is missing," Skuli announced. "That might have something to do with it."

"Missing?" Sigmund asked. "Is he completely gone?"

That question mystified most of the Volsungs, but Skuli
seemed to understand.

"There is no trace of blood, although I do smell it
faintly," he answered. "I suspect that someone tried their
best to wash it away."

Sigmund sat in silence for a moment, deep in thought.
Skuli's report was an accurate one, for taking human form
compromised only slightly their wolfish sense of smell.
"It was the wolf. Now I understand the full nature of
Siggier's revenge."

"A wolf would not have attacked us," Sorli protested.
To the Volsungs, that suggested more than just murder,
but cannibalism. "Not for any reason. Not unless Siggier
has tortured it to the point of madness . . . which I can
readily accept."

"The wolf I saw was as big as a pony," Sigmund
explained. "A wolf of Jotunheim, possibly even a landvaeta
possessed by some evil spirit. Siggier did mention to me
that his friend has supplied him with some very special
spies. It looks like what we would call a wolf, but I claim
no kin to it."

"But why a wolf?" Kari insisted, still revolted by the
idea.

"Simply more of Siggier's vengeance. He either suspected the effect that it would have upon us, or he simply
liked the irony."

A few minutes later a number of warriors, almost a
small army, arrived. They set about their assigned tasks,
never speaking a word, and the Volsungs neither said nor
asked anything in return. The Volsungs were released from
their bonds and, one by one, taken under heavy escort into
the woods to attend their morning duties. Afterwards they
were fed, not the usual short rations of a prisoner but
venison and cheese such as wolflings preferred. They could
not imagine why their captor would show any consider-

ation for their welfare, rather than allow them to suffer hunger and thirst as they awaited their deaths.

The guards returned late that afternoon with dinner, again never speaking a word. Night fell slowly, and the wolflings waited in anticipation. Darkness was only just complete when they began to feel the sleeping spell taking effect once again, and they fought the magic in vain. They were still awake enough to be aware of the great wolf as it came and stood waiting patiently.

CHAPTER EIGHT

Again the Volsungs began to awaken almost in the same instant. Their first awareness was that they had survived the night; their first question was to ask who had not. Sigmund was not surprised to find himself alive, for he knew that Siggier was saving him. Kari had also been left, for Sigmund could hear his younger brother swearing just as on the previous morning, if somewhat less loudly. But a second set of stocks would be empty, and he was by no means eager to discover which.

"Sorli is gone," Halvard announced from the other side of the line of stocks. By reporting that quickly he had brought a swift answer to that terrible question, and the Volsungs were free to breath somewhat easier.

"Does it seem the same as before?" Sigmund asked.

"Yes, as far as I can tell," Halvard replied. "There is not a trace of what might have happened, not even the smell of blood."

"I smell something," Ragnar, at the very end, remarked. "Blood, perhaps. But also some strange beast, such as I have never smelled before. That must be the Jotunheim wolf. It was likely standing right beside me."

"You have a keener nose," Halvard admitted. "I do not smell either."

"Today we are going to think a way out of this trap," Sigmund said forcefully, to distract the others from their thoughts.

"I do recall hearing mortal trappers tell of animals that have bitten off a paw to free themselves from a trap," Kari remarked.

Bren laughed. "There are just two problems with that. If you bite off your own paws, how do you expect to free the rest of us? And I doubt that you can bite your head off to free it, and that would do you even less good if you did."

"I was not considering that as a suggestion!" Kari snapped, stung into more serious thought. "The real problem is that we have the strength to free ourselves, but bent over like this we are not in a position to use that strength effectively. In short, our problem is one of leverage."

"That seems a fair assumption," Sigmund agreed, since he had thought of that a day earlier. "Do you see any solutions to that problem?"

"It seems to me that if one of us could free his shoulders and straighten his back, then he could apply the full strength of his shoulders toward breaking the hinges of the stocks," Kari said. That was a promising thought. They all had massive shoulder muscles, developed from running in their true forms.

"But we need our hands to free our heads," Keldan pointed out.

"I wonder if we might be able to free our heads in our true forms," Kari suggested. "Wolves have a smaller brain case than humans, and the shape of the wolf's head is more horizontal and elongated."

"I, or perhaps Bren, am about the largest of us all in wolf form," Sigmund said. "You, Kari, are the smallest—in either form. The runt of the litter, if I might say so."

There were a few chuckles, much to Kari's annoyance.

"The point is that you are the most likely to be able to slip through. Try it cautiously. Just remember that your neck is the most narrow at the top, so try drawing your head back as far as you can before you change."

Kari nodded, then took a deep breath and converted. There was no problem about the hole being too small, crushing his thicker wolf's neck. He completed the conversion just as he began to draw back, and the opening was wide enough for his neck to pass through easily. Easily enough, in fact, for him to crack his head sharply. He grunted, dazed, then made some deep growling noises like a continuation of his usual swearing.

"Try it again!" Skuli said encouragingly. "You might crack the board!"

Kari glared at him, then stuck out a long wolf's tongue and made a rude sound. He paused a moment to collect himself, then closed his eyes and slowly drew back his head. He was able to draw back up to his ears, but no farther. He shook and shifted his head, hoping to force his way back a little bit more, but to no effect. At last he gave up and sat panting.

"I was afraid of that," Sigmund said.

"The problem is my ears," Kari said, his wolf's voice just noticeably lower than his normal tenor. "Perhaps, with enough force, they will fold enough for me to succeed."

"Do not hurt yourself," Sigmund warned.

"Worth it!" Kari said, smiling grimly. "Even if I have to leave my ears behind. I simply cannot get enough leverage; far less, in this form, than in human. Wolves simply were not made for sitting on a bench."

He carefully set his forelegs against the sides of the stock, testing his hold, and renewed his struggles to extract his head. His muffled grunts and whines indicated the amount of effort he was putting into this attempt, but to no effect. The problem, as he had said, remained one of leverage. He was in no real danger of damaging his ears; he was finally forced to admit that his head simply was not going through that hole, ears or no ears. But he spent the rest of the day trying everything he could think of, until the coming of night and the spell of sleep put an end to his struggles.

The wolflings awoke the next morning without the usual assault of curses, for Kari was gone. And, for the first time, Sigmund wept, for his youngest brother had also been his most beloved. But he did learn one important thing from it. For the wolf of Jotunheim had not selected his victim entirely at random. As he had suspected from the first, Siggier had some way of spying upon them, or at least their words. And Kari, who possessed a fair portion of his sister's sharp wit and wisdom, had been removed before he did indeed find a way to escape. But he also began to hope that Siggier could be defeated, if Kari had been that close to discovering how.

Sigmund had more faith in his ability to free himself than in the chance that Signy might find a way to free him. He did not doubt her abilities; he knew that she was wiser than himself, and far more likely to find a way out of this trap. He also assumed that she was under much heavier guard than himself, either confined to the main hall or imprisoned outright.

Signy was indeed under constant guard and restricted to the main hall. She did have the advantage of knowing all the traps Siggier had laid out to guard his prisoners; her only problem was how to make use of that knowledge. But she had one important advantage that she was not aware of. For Brynhild the Valkyrie was with her a great deal of the time, unseen and unnoticed, waiting for the opportunity to shape circumstances to the wolfling's favor. Signy, of course, was unaware of her invisible helper and was frustrated with trying to solve her problems for herself.

Brynhild was nearly as frustrated, since despite her greater freedom, the Allfather's very exact orders gave her very little freedom to act. However she could contrive the Volsungs' escape, it had to appear to be entirely their own doing, which effectively prevented her from taking any direct actions. After considering the problem carefully, Brynhild decided that the only option was to help Signy rescue her brothers. If Signy had but one key, she had the courage and intelligence to unlock all their traps. The problem was finding just such a key and getting it into her hands.

Days passed only too swiftly, but the Valkyrie was becoming quite deft at playing upon Siggier's subconscious will. This was, in fact, a very easy task, since for all his crafty intelligence and the magic that he received from the Jotnar, he did not possess a trace of power of his own. She could not force him to spare or release the Volsungs, for his will was too firmly set on that matter. But by her intervention, he kept Signy very well informed on the state of the prisoners and the nature of his traps and safeguards, and a great many other things that he would have otherwise spoken to no one.

So it was, on the day after the eighth night, Siggier was entertaining himself by admiring the magical devices and spells that he had received from Utgardh-Loki, when he was possessed by a sudden urge to check on Signy. He had recently come to a decision that had been bothering him for days, and since it meant her life he was mindful to tell her of it. As much as anything he simply wanted to see her. He wanted to be reminded of her wolfish traits, of her gray mane, her dark, elvish features and curious eyes, her animal litheness. The very things about her that he actually found the most attractive . . . at least the most fascinating.

And he was so distracted that he failed to notice that he still bore one of the peeled wands that carried the sleeping spell.

He entered, as always, without knocking, startling both Signy and her ever-present guards. She paused where she was, staring back at him in wild bemusement like some animal caught in the open in the bare instant before it leaped for cover. She seemed the most wolfish then, and it suddenly occurred to him that he had never seen her in her true form. Now, perhaps, he just might, for his wand of mistletoe could force the change. After a moment she straightened her back, affecting a more human pose.

"I was on my way back from tending your brothers," he said, motioning the guards out of the room. "Or, rather, your brother."

"Only Sigmund remains?" she asked.

"I always did intend to save him for the last," Siggier admitted. "There is some chance that the Wanderer will finally give in and allow me the magic sword, in which case he is welcome to you both. But I doubt it, and I will not spare Sigmund."

He paused a moment and laid the wand on the high wooden chest that stood beside the door. He did not notice as the slender length of wood suddenly rolled to fall off the edge of the chest between it and the wall. But Signy saw this and did her best to remain composed.

"You, however, need not worry. I expect to keep you, for a while yet, at least," Siggier continued. "I am mindful now of why I wanted you. I wanted a wolfling son, a son of extraordinary abilities. True, you have given me two sons, but I know as well as you that they are quite mortal. Give me another son, a wolfling son. The last Volsung, to inherit my kingdom."

He walked slowly over to her and stared down at her, standing a head and a half above her tiny form. She was prepared for the revulsion she always felt under his possessive gaze, and she was surprised to see a rare look of gentleness and even sorrow in his eyes.

"I know what you want," he said. "Where you most want to be. Grant me this one wish. Give me a wolfling son, and I promise—and this promise you can trust—that I will let you go. You have all time ahead of you, so I know that another year means nothing to you."

"The years pass slowly for me," she answered. "More so, when you keep me trapped like a beast in a cage."

"You will have a little more freedom now," Siggier told her. "There is nothing now you can do, for the game will be ended tonight. The guards will remain outside your doors from now on."

He turned then to leave, taking no notice of the wand that had fallen behind the chest. But he paused at the door.

"I will come when I am ready for you," he added, looking back at her. "Not yet."

Signy had to leave the wand where it had fallen until that evening in the event that Siggier recalled that he had forgotten it and returned. But once the light of day began to fade, she fetched the wand from behind the chest and began to probe its secrets. The wolflings were not unlearned in the lore of magic, and Signy had made it a special study, having some powers of her own. She immediately recognized the spell this wand contained and how she could make it work for her. Thus she had two keys; a weapon to free herself and her twin, and the new freedom to use it.

She quickly removed her clothing, knowing that her small, brown body would be better hidden in the darkness than any mortal clothing, then went to the door and listened carefully through the crack. There were two guards outside, seated on a bench to one side of the door; she did not need to see them to be aware of that. She aimed the wand in their direction and softly spoke the words in invocation and listened as their breathing became soft and regular. Then she hurried to the outer wall. The windows were barred against her passage, but she had some new magic of her own to serve her now. She leaned against the wall, pressing herself to it as firmly as she could. In the next instant she passed through its very substance and emerged on the outside in her wolfish form.

Signy looked about and tested the wind with her nose and knew that there was no one about. And so she ran north into the forest, fleet and as silent as the shadows. But soon she slowed and made her way stealthily. There were guards about the stocks, dark elves who could see into the night as easily as herself, but she came up behind them. She took the wand from between her teeth and aimed it in their direction. A moment later they slept as well. She shifted into her wolf form and hurried on.

She found the clearing not far beyond, the row of stocks empty save for one. Smiling with excitement and delight, she trotted up to Sigmund and stood staring at him. He stared back at her.

"Are you the replacement?" he asked. "You are a bit small, and you are early . . . I am not yet asleep. I certainly hope that you do not think that you can eat me by yourself. And you could at least have the decency not to grin and wag your tail."

Signy blinked. "Sigmund, it is me. Your sister."

"Don't you think I know that?" he asked. "Now bring the key and get me out of here."

"I don't have the key," she said, changing into human form. "All I have is one of Siggier's sleep-spell wands."

Sigmund looked into his sister's face for the first time in many years. He could not see much in the light of a half-moon, only large eyes gleaming from behind a shock of gray hair and a warm smile that was gentle and reassuring. She seemed so confident and calm that he felt inclined to trust her.

"Have you ever thought of what happens to you when you change from one form to another?" she asked. "Do you think that you simply become a wolf, or do you actually exchange bodies, one for another?"

"It must be the latter, from the way you phrased that."

"Precisely," she agreed. "That is the sort of thing I am always wondering about. Once, to test this idea, I held a large, flat rock in my paws when I changed form. My hands were in exactly the same place, but the rock slipped through."

"Paws are more clumsy than hands," Sigmund remarked uncertainly.

"Then answer me something even simpler," Signy challenged. "If you only turn from one to another, then why are you not still wearing your clothes? Where do they go? They always come back."

"Yours did not," he reminded her, and frowned. "Then we have two bodies, and the other is always somewhere else until we need it?"

"And for just an instant you are nowhere."

Sigmund blinked in bemusement. "The idea of being nowhere for an instant does not bother me as much as the thought that there must be a closet somewhere holding my unused body as if it were a change of clothes."

Signy laughed. "There is no time to argue the point. Listen to me. Whatever the cause, I have made it work for me. For an instant, that instant that you are nowhere, you can pass through solid objects."

"What?" he demanded in disbelief.

"How do you think I got away tonight?" she asked in return. "You are not practiced in this, so we will begin

with just one hand. Try to draw it straight up out of the top
of the stock at the same instant that you change forms.''

"You realize what might happen if my hand material-
izes inside the wood?'' he asked.

"I took the risk for the sake of knowledge. Can you not
take the same risk to save your life?''

"A good point,'' Sigmund agreed and did as she directed, only to become a wolf with two firmly trapped
paws. He quickly converted back. "That does settle two
important questions. It is possible. I felt it give, but then
the wood kicked it forward again as my paw materialized.
And that means that I cannot materialize inside the wood.''

He tried again, and this time as he became a wolf, his
paw slipped through so easily that he threw himself off-
balance. Signy caught him and pushed him back up, and
an instant later he returned to human form. He was about
to try with the other hand when he paused.

"Signy, we just ran out of time,'' he said softly. "The
wolf is coming.''

"Hurry,'' she urged. "I cannot fight him alone.''

"Do not worry about it,'' Sigmund assured her. "I
cannot get out of here in time, but I have a plan. You hide
yourself, but stay ready.''

Signy did as he directed, retreating to the cover of the
nearest bush and crouching down behind it to watch, ready
to spring to her brother's defense. Sigmund listened to her
movements, unable to turn his head to see, then glanced
up to the forest beyond to see a dim shape approaching out
of the shadows. He quickly put his free hand back to the
empty hole and, ignoring the extreme discomfort, hung his
head limply as if asleep.

The wolf stepped out of the shadows, heedless of any
caution after nine previous uneventful raids, and trotted
directly up to the stocks. One more night and then this
unpleasant business would be finished, and he could return

home. This night he caught another scent, a second wolf-ish scent, all about this end of the stocks. Though possessing demonic intelligence, he did not possess the wit to understand this matter. He only knew that the other wolf-lings were dead, and there was no creature for him to fear in this world anyway. He moved in, opening his powerful jaws to bite through the neck of his prey.

At that moment a fist seemed to come out of nowhere, connecting with his jaw hard enough to break it with a loud snap. For just an instant, startled and confused, the wolf only stood and blinked. Then just as the first wave of intense pain exploded within his jaw, that same arm encir-cled his neck and pinned it tight. The wolf began to struggle, unable to pull free for all his size and strength. He jerked and thrashed wildly in his confusion and grow-ing fear.

Then a set of sharp teeth closed upon his tail, crushing the delicate bones. He froze, wide-eyed as pain ran as a visible shiver up his spine. He howled, piercingly sharp, and thrashed with the strength of ten Jotunish wolves. The stock exploded in splinters, and the smaller wolf attached to his tail was thrown over the stock to land on the far side of the clearing. But the larger wolf, howling and yelping as much in terror as in pain, did not even look back as he bolted for the safety of the forest. His tortured howls continued to drift back through the night for some time to come.

CHAPTER NINE

Sigmund suppressed a groan as he sat up. His arm felt as if it had been dislocated at the shoulder, and his neck was painfully stiff and half again as long as it should be. He had been hurled backwards off the bench by the force that had eventually freed him. The upper portion of his own stock was hanging by its twisted hinge; the wood along either side had broken free of the locking mechanism and the long bolts that had secured it. Looking at it, he was surprised that his bones had been stronger than the wood.

He rose and looked about, recalling that his sister had given a hand—or a mouth—in his rescue. He saw her at last, lying on her side in the deep grass a great deal farther away than he had anticipated. She simply lay there unmoving, and just when he was becoming concerned, she converted back to human form and sat up, holding her head. She sat and glared at him as he walked over to her, so that he grinned sheepishly.

"That was your plan?" she asked incredulously.

Sigmund shrugged helplessly. "Simple, but effective."

Signy only rolled her eyes and lay back in the grass, then quickly sat up again and spat long, gray hairs from the wolf's tail. The ridiculousness of it all caught up with

Sigmund then, and he sat down beside her and laughed. Signy was in no mood to share the humor, however, and only glared at him even harder.

"Well, what do we do now?" she insisted. "We are alone in the world, with nowhere to go. Do you have any idea of what we should do?"

Sigmund sat and thought about that for a moment. "No, I do not. We cannot return home, and I do not know where the world-gate is. All the Volsungs are dead or gone away, so we can count upon no help. Not even the Wanderer can help us now."

"The Wanderer has already helped us," Signy said. "He came the first night, and he tricked Siggier into sinking your sword up to its hilt in a tree. It awaits you still. Also he helped me gain possession of this, or so I believe. A magic wand, keyed to a sleep spell."

"But why has the Wanderer suddenly become so reluctant to act openly on our behalf?" Sigmund demanded. "He has always been quick to help the wolflings before. If he had acted, our brothers would still be alive."

"How can I judge such matters?" Signy asked in return. "If I must hazard a wild guess for your satisfaction, then I would say that it touches upon that mysterious task our race was created to complete. A task that the great ones of Asgardh cannot complete themselves, or else they must remain circumspect in the matter."

Sigmund looked up at her, and she nodded. "I wonder if that time has come, that Siggier and his friends may release some great evil into this world that you must destroy. Something they cannot face, but you can because we were made to be immune to its powers."

"Me?" Sigmund asked, so startled—and afraid—that he could think of no better response.

"Yes, you," Signy insisted. "You were given the sword

so that all will be ready for you to complete the task when the time comes. You, or your child.''

He glanced at her, startled. ''I have no child.''

''Not yet,'' she corrected him gently.

She rose first and held out her hand to him. He started to reach up with his right hand to take hers, only to find that he could not move it. When he tried, he had to catch his breath to keep from crying out. Signy quickly dropped down beside him and began to inspect his shoulder cautiously.

''It is dislocated, of course,'' she decided. ''Nor am I surprised. It is a wonder, in fact, that you did not break your neck. Did you not know?''

''Everything hurt so much at first, I couldn't tell just what might have been twisted or broken.''

''There is no help for it now,'' Signy said briskly. ''I will be quick, but you should find yourself a tree to hold on to.''

Sigmund looked around the clearing for a likely tree. The next instant Signy took firm hold of his arm and twisted the shoulder back into place. Caught by surprise, Sigmund chose two of Kari's favorite oaths and used them to effect.

''Sorry about that,'' Signy said. ''I've always heard that it is better if you do not expect it.''

''I cannot say that it does anything to lessen the pain,'' he replied. ''Just the anxiety.''

''Well, you certainly will not be pulling any sword tonight,'' Signy said. ''I suppose that the only thing we can do is for you to hide out in the forest for a few days. I will go back and distract Siggier from looking for you. I can play my role for a few more days.''

Even the less mobile ears Sigmund wore in mortal form lifted in amazement. ''Signy, you cannot go back. Siggier will have your hide, and in truth, once he discovers what has happened.''

''And what has happened?'' she countered. ''As well as Siggier can tell, you are dead. Perhaps the wolf tore up the stock to get you out. Perhaps he came in before the spell had taken effect, and there was a fight. Either way, the wolf is gone and you are gone. And do not worry about me. Siggier has become suddenly enamored with me . . . due, I suspect, to the Wanderer's subtle encouragement.''

Sigmund considered that for a moment. He did not like the idea, but he could see that he was not going to talk her out of it. ''Very well. I will find a place in the forest north of here. Come to me in three nights, and then we may be able to tell just how soon I will be able to travel.''

''Three nights,'' she agreed, collecting the wand. ''Leave a trail that I can follow by scent.''

The Allfather was alone in the study of his mansion, reading through a lengthy message from the elfking. He glanced up expectantly as Brynhild entered, striding purposefully in without even the courtesy of knocking. But seeing the dark scowl she wore, he paused and looked concerned.

''Did the wolflings fail?'' he asked.

''Oh, no! They are alive and well enough,'' Brynhild said, flipping aside her cape as she eased her armored form into a large chair opposite his own. ''But Signy refused to go. She returned to Siggier's holding.''

Odhinn sat up straight. ''She what? Is that little fool going to throw away her own life?''

''No, perhaps not,'' Brynhild said, although she did not sound certain. ''She did her best to arrange matters so that Siggier will believe that Sigmund is dead. And she still has the wand.''

''Then she must be planning something.''

"Her problem is that she's entirely too devoted to duty. She will not leave without the sword, but Sigmund has dislocated his shoulder and cannot draw it. When he is well enough, she probably plans to use her wand on the entire hall so he can return for it. Also, I sense that she is reluctant to leave her children."

"Can you not understand that?" Odhinn asked. "Still, her mortal children are worthless to her. She must mate with Sigmund."

"She intends to."

"Then what is the problem?" Odhinn asked.

"She has also arrived at the ridiculous theory that the task you have set for them is to slay some terrible magical presence that Siggier will import from Jotunheim."

Odhinn sat back and made a derisive sound. "Does she think that I can foresee the future? As much as I would like. . . ."

"You are a god," Brynhild reminded him.

He glanced up at her. "The Volsungs know better."

"Perhaps they do not sacrifice goats to win your favor, but even Signy gives you credit for limited omnipotence. And she believes that you are helping her."

"Then you must see that she gets the help she needs," Odhinn said. "Insure that Siggier does not suspect, and she will do the rest. And do not forget your other duties. You have the rest of the night to complete your regular patrol."

"Have I ever failed in my duty?" Brynhild asked as she jumped up, grinning broadly. Permission to help the Volsungs was all she wanted, although Odhinn's renewed interest in their well-being delighted her more.

"Where are you going in such a hurry?" Odhinn asked as she headed for the door, amused with her determination.

"To slay that broken-jawed wolf of Jotunheim!" she

called back. "If he comes sneaking back whining for help, he could ruin everything."

The door slammed behind her, leaving Odhinn to sit in bemused reflection and wishing that he had asked for more details. He dearly wanted to know how the wolf of Jotunheim had come to have a broken jaw. So much for omnipotence.

Signy stole away into the night at the appointed time, running in wolf form. She quickly caught her brother's scent and traced him to a den he had made for himself inside a wide overhang of stone that had at some time been made into a hunter's hut. The wood of the outer wall and door were in an advanced state of decay but still sound enough for the short time that he would be there. He was himself living in wolf form, even though his shoulder still pained him. Without the tools and weapons that mortal men needed to survive in the wild, he was better off in that form.

He had been doing a great deal of careful thinking since the last time they had met, trying to make some decision about their own future and that of their race. Now he had some very difficult questions to ask.

"Signy," he said softly as they sat side by side in the moonlight before the door of his lodge. "Are you certain that your children are not Volsung?"

She looked at him, bewildered, even accusing. "They were born mortal. They act and think mortal. They are Siggier's children, not my own."

"I do not want this to be difficult for you," he said apologetically. "But if they are wolflings, then we are that much farther ahead. We must know. But if they are, then their true natures are hidden very deeply indeed. The only way I know to force that part of themselves to the surface—if it even exists—is in the face of certain death. The inner parts of their minds will know if they are wolflings, and call upon that part to save their lives.''

"You would kill my children if they are mortal?'' Signy asked, although more questioningly than in indignation. Then she seemed to find her own answer to that and looked away. "No, you are right. If they are true Volsungs, then I would not leave them here. If they are mortal, then they are their father's sons, and this world is better off without two more of his kind.''

"Are you sure?'' Sigmund asked gently. "I will not force this.''

"Sigmund, they are not my children. Siggier has never allowed me near them. Days or even weeks pass without my ever seeing them, and I have certainly never had the opportunity to so much as speak to them. They do not even regard me as their mother; as with everyone else, they know me only as that half-tame wolf girl their father keeps.''

So it was decided. The next day Sigmund trapped a wild wolf inside his den and kept her there for many days, until she was half mad with frustration and hunger. When all was ready, Signy slipped out of her room by night, armed with her wand and the ability to transport herself through walls. She circled the hall until she found the proper window, then checked inside to insure that she had made no mistake. The window was locked against her, but she ran now in her true form. She leaned against the wall and then leaped forward as she felt herself beginning to phase through, and the next instant she was standing inside the room in human form.

She hesitated a moment, wondering which of the two boys to wake first. Geir was the oldest, now in his ninth year, and perhaps less likely to be frightened by the sudden appearance in the middle of the night of someone he did not know well. And yet young Thrain, only in his sixth year, might be less prejudiced against her by the gossip of his nurses. Choosing mostly at random, she went to Geir's bed and gently shook him awake.

Geir stirred and looked up at her. "What is it? Haldris?"

"I am Signy, your mother," she answered softly. "You must be very quiet. You must go with me into the forest tonight, and no one must know."

"Why?" he asked in the suspicious, calculating voice she associated with his father.

"You know what I am?" she asked, and he nodded slowly. "Well, I am your mother, and what I am might be you in part. If you are wolfling, then we must find that out quickly. Your life depends upon it."

"But I was not born a wolf," the boy protested. "My father. . . ."

"Your father hates the Volsungs," Signy interrupted him. "He hates the wolflings so much that he would risk your life, and that of your brother, rather than admit that you might be wolfling by putting you to the test. I will put you to the test, and your father will never know. But you must come very quietly."

Geir considered that for a long moment and nodded slowly; fortunately, he was still young enough to be gullible.

"Then wake your brother and get yourself ready to go," she instructed. "Do not tell your brother that his life depends upon it; he is too young. Tell him only that it is very important, and that no one must know."

Signy led them to a small clearing some distance from Sigmund's forest dwelling. Her brother had shown her the place, saying that should her children fail the test, then their screams would not be heard either in the holding or here where the second might yet wait. It was not, however, far enough for her sharp ears to miss those sounds, and she was grateful that she did not have to be anywhere near the place itself. She heard her brother coming long before he appeared and quickly called the children to where she sat on a fallen log.

"The time has come," she told them. "One of my people has come to lead the first of you to the place of testing."

"Your people are dead," Geir protested.

"No, your father is mistaken," she said. "Many of my race, even I do not know how many, live as wolves in the elfrealm. This one will take you to the place of testing. You must go with him, and do as he tells you."

"You will not come?" Thrain asked.

"No, I cannot. I will await you here." She paused and looked at each of them. "Geir, I think that you should go first."

Geir nodded, then straightened his shoulders and turned to join Sigmund, waiting patiently at the head of the path. That was the hardest moment for Signy, knowing that it was her last chance to stop this game, and knowing as well that she could not. Instead she sat and watched him go until tears filled her eyes, not for the son she was certain to lose, but for the son who had never been her own. Then she smiled reassuringly at Thrain and ruffled his hair, for at the very least she would not have him distressed.

Sigmund hurried back to his forest dwelling, for dawn was approaching too swiftly for all that remained to be done. Geir bravely tried to match his quick pace without running, but Sigmund soon slowed somewhat, realizing that it would be unfair to put him to this test winded. At least the boy faced the challenge courageously, saying nothing and asking no questions, as if this were a simple task quickly done. They paused for a moment when they came within sight of the hut, and Sigmund crouched down to speak with the boy.

"Beneath that pile of stones is a hunter's dwelling. Do

you see it?'' he asked, and waited for the boy to nod. ''There is a door in the front and an opening in the top. I want you to drop down through that opening. There is a fire inside, so you will be able to see.

''From this point on, you must concentrate upon being a wolf. Make yourself believe that you are a wolf. Then, when you see what is within the dwelling, the wolf within you will prove itself. Remember that it is nothing that a wolf would ever be afraid of. When you are done, leave by the door. Go now.''

Geir turned without a word and strode purposefully out onto the roof, then lowered himself carefully through the opening. The moment he disappeared inside, the fierce snarling and growling of an enraged wolf filled the night. Geir screamed once, a long, despairing scream that was suddenly cut off as powerful jaws closed about his throat.

Sigmund sighed heavily and retrieved the body before the wolf could begin to feed. Then he returned for Thrain, but the younger boy fared no better. Sigmund took no satisfaction in seeing that the wolf had bitten off their heads just as Siggier had ordered done with his own brothers. Vengeance for their deaths was ever in his mind, but vengeance only against Siggier himself, not against two trusting children. He buried their bodies and hid the graves beneath mouldering leaves, then fed the starving wolf a haunch he had saved and left the door open for her. Heavy of heart, he returned to Signy a final time.

She looked up at him expectantly as he stepped into the clearing, and he saw that she had been weeping. He pitied her then, but admired her as well for her resolve. She rose slowly as he approached, nervously smoothing the folds of her robe although she never took her eyes form his.

''It is actually a relief, now that it is over,'' she said in an unsteady voice. ''They were not my children, and I do not grieve for them. I only hate what I needed to do. Did . . . did they die well?"

"They faced the challenge bravely, without hesitation or complaint," he answered. "And they died swiftly, with little pain or fear. But they were not wolflings. There was never any question."

"No, no question, but it had to be done," Signy said quickly, shaking her head. Then she looked up at him. "There is nothing more to be done. When will you be able to pull the sword?"

"Any time now," he assured her. "But I am not yet ready to haul a sail or fight a tiller. Can you give me another five days?"

"Easy enough. That will give me time to prepare supplies for our journey. I will come for you that night."

Sigmund nodded, then took her in his arms and held her tightly against him for a long moment. Then he let her go, and she turned and slowly walked away, back toward the holding.

"Signy?" he asked urgently. "Can you go back, this time?"

She turned to look at him. "Do not worry about me. I know how to arrange matters, as I did before."

CHAPTER TEN

It seemed to Signy that she had hardly closed her eyes before Siggier charged through her door, throwing it against the wall with a reverberating crack. She tried to track him with ears that refused to move and became aware, with a sudden stab of icy fear, that he was raging over the disappearance of their children. Then she began to realize that he was not raging at her but only continued to spit out curses and threats between his demands for her to do something. Siggier paused when he saw her puzzled look, and, realizing that she had not heard a word, he descended upon her like an enraged dragon.

"I said that your children are gone!" he repeated as he snatched the cover from her and all but lifted her out of bed. "Kidnapped, or worse! Come and put your long nose to this puzzle."

"I cannot," she mumbled as he pushed her toward the door. "My clothes."

Siggier paused, turning her around and looking her up and down, as if becoming aware of her nakedness for the first time. For a moment he seemed startled by that sight; he liked women soft and shapely, while she was wiry and rippling with firm muscle. Like all wolflings in mortal form, her thick mane extended down to the base of her spine, causing her to look even more unhuman.

"Forget that," he said irritably. "Put on your wolf skin. It's that nose of yours that I want anyway."

Signy dropped to all fours as she shifted to her true form and paced before Siggier as he herded her down the hall. As she neared the room that had been occupied by her children, she encountered increasing numbers of warriors standing about, ready for battle but finding none. She was pleased to see everyone give way before her, for she was descended of the great wolves of the Vargarbraut, as large and intimidating in this form as she was small and delicate in mortal form.

Signy began to slow as they neared the door, knowing what to expect and preparing herself for the proper reactions of surprise and concern. She had carefully laid a false trail the night before, knowing that Siggier would have his landvaetir on it immediately. She had not expected this.

Siggier nudged her in the rump as she paused just short of the door.

She looked up at him. "Death has been here."

"Not your children," Siggier said. "Not here, at least. Find me a trail, and I will find them or avenge them."

A single body lay inside the door, Haldris the nurse, strangled so forcefully that her neck was broken. Haldris, when ten years younger and her lord's plaything, had been wet nurse to Geir at the same time she cared for her bastard, for Siggier had not allowed his all-too-human son wolfling milk. Signy leaped the body and began to pace the room, as if hunting any odd scent.

"Well?" Siggier asked impatiently.

"Too many scents." Signy paused to look at him. "You have let too many strangers in this room."

"Does that make any difference to your snout?"

"I am not a hound!" Signy snapped, then lifted her

muzzle to sniff again. "Someone in this room smelled strongly of swine."

"Swine?" Siggier asked incredulously.

"Too strongly. I would say that they disguised their scents with swineherd's clothes, unless perhaps you know of any pig-riders."

Siggier snorted in derisive amusement at the thought of hog-riding warriors raiding his holding. Signy did not pause, but traced the scent to the window and promptly hopped out. Soldiers, gathered outside, scurried out of the way apprehensively, but she paid them no heed as she sought out the trail and followed it along the side of the hall and on toward the woods, nearly a quarter of a mile, until she came to a stream. She knew where she had tied the rags to pieces of wood to float down the stream to the sea, hardly a mile away. But she crossed the area repeatedly, carefully confusing the trail.

Then, for good measure, she followed the path back again, weaving back and forth and crossing the trail many times to hide the fact that she had made this journey not once but three times. The next nose to follow that track would trace only two swineherds and the two children, the overlaying scent of wolf due to her own careful tracing hours later. Satisfied that she had done all she could, she returned, leaping back through the window.

Siggier stood leaning against the doorframe, patiently awaiting her return. "So?"

Signy sat back on her haunches to look up at him. "Two pig-riders came from the stream, and took the children back along the same path. Their trail begins and ends in the stream. I assume that they waded in and out by the stream, from where a boat waited for them in the cove. Some clue might be had from exploring the beach, but I doubt it. They probably waded right out of their boat, so that they left no scent or other trace."

"The children were alive?"

"I certainly smelled no blood."

"And no prints?"

"The ground is hard."

"Not that hard," Siggier said and indicated the body. "Whoever did that was strong. As strong as myself, and likely as big."

"The ground is hard. There are no tracks," Signy repeated, which fortunately was the truth. Like most wolflings, she never wore shoes, and a small, slender bare print would have been remarkable.

Siggier did not reply. A moment later an immense weasel, twice normal size, squeezed between his legs, only to stop short as he spied Signy sitting on the far side of the room by the window. The landvaeta immediately arched his long back and hissed fiercely. Signy only regarded it with polite interest.

Siggier, startled by that unexpected reaction, booted the weasel in the rump. "Stop that, Trigin. This is my wife, Signy Sigisdottir of the Volsungs, so mind your manners."

"Wife?" Trigin piped and shook his triangular head slowly as he regarded the wolfling. "Mixed marriages."

Trigin began with the body, a task Signy had disdained, and even disappeared into the folds of the nurse's long gown to check for signs of rape. Licking his chops disgustingly, he continued on about the room. At last he edged cautiously around the placid wolf and slithered out the window.

"Nasty little beast," Signy remarked.

"Trigin is just more animal than you are," Siggier replied.

She looked at him closely. "You do not seem greatly upset by the disappearance of your sons."

"No more than yourself, if not for the same reason. Avenging the deed is now my only concern," he admitted frankly, then saw her look at him. "In fact, it does solve a problem I have been anticipating. Soon you will give me the son I want, and I intend for him to inherit all I have built. Him alone."

"Geir and Thrain were problems to be eliminated should you have a wolfling son?" Signy deduced, too fascinated to be dismayed. Trigin was not the only weasel in this holding.

"Problems that are now solved," Siggier corrected her, then glanced at her. "Whatever their fates, they will not return home alive."

Signy suppressed a shudder, not for hearing his murderous plans, but for the realization that she had beat him to the act and had throttled their nurse for good measure.

"I did not intend for my holding to be broken up anyway," Siggier continued. "Only one was to inherit. There is an old trick, that a father should encourage a winner-take-all situation among his sons, so that the . . . survivor, the most capable and ruthless, would take all."

"And the best would one day pay you the greatest honor yet by putting something in your cup?" Signy asked wryly.

Siggier stared at her for a moment, then laughed heartily. "Yes, indeed! If any son of mine could put that over on me, then he deserves my kingdom. But I have already proven myself quite difficult to kill."

"There have been attempts?"

"Seven since you first came," he said. "And I doubt that you were even aware of a single one. The rumor is quite true; I did fight my mother to the death for possession of this holding. The one point in my favor is that she nearly got me first. She did get my father, the only time he was ever vulnerable to her . . . when they were making love."

"Crude, but effective. I must remember that."

Siggier regarded her again. "You know, I think I like

you better as a wolf. You are more interesting . . . easier
to talk to.''

He looked up as the weasel returned, scrabbling over the
sill and then tumbling with an alarmed squeak to the floor.
He rose slowly and made quite a show of popping every
joint in his long back, grunting with delight at each. Then
he sat down with a sigh of relief.

"Well?" Siggier asked.

Trigin shrugged. "I followed the trail to the end. Your
sons were taken by a pair of marauding pigs, then a wolf
came along later and muddled up the trail good. You really
should follow that stream down to the bay.''

"You follow it!" Siggier snapped and looked over his
shoulder. "Thorvald, take a party of warriors and assist
this vermin in a careful search of the stream all the way
down to the bay. And do have the corpse taken away.
Signy, my dear, would you care to dress for breakfast?''

Signy would not have worried so, had it occurred to her
that she was still receiving careful and almost continuous
help. Brynhild had been with her in spirit, unseen, throughout every step of her unpleasant night. Delighted with her
deft handling of the matter, Brynhild recalled her projected
consciousness back to her body, seated beneath a tree
under Glaerfaxi's careful watch. She opened her eyes and
nearly jumped out of her armor when she saw Odhinn
seated not four paces away, watching her intently.

"So, you return triumphant after a fruitful night of
meddling," he said, and there was no mistaking his anger.
"Do you know how close you brought the whole affair to
disaster? If you or those foolish wolflings had made a
single mistake in the double net of deception you have
been weaving, it would have cost Signy her life.''

"It did not," Brynhild replied defensively. "I knew
exactly what I was doing.''

"Then kindly explain what purpose it served. You had both of those wolflings functioning well outside their instinctive behavior, with Signy leading her own children to the slaughter and Sigmund carrying out the execution. If you had not been successful in making them believe the rightness and necessity of their acts, you could have damaged their minds."

"Signy could not forget her children."

"She was willing to leave them behind," Odhinn countered.

"I saw in her mind that she wanted to take them with her," Brynhild said. "That would have been certain disaster."

"You could have easily put the idea out of her mind."

"That is true, certainly," she admitted. "I trusted my instincts. . . ."

"You are a spirit of power," Odhinn answered softly, coldly. "You have no instincts. You did what might have been right for you. Even a true human might have maintained such detachment for unwanted children, even hate. But Signy is of a hybred race of dire wolves who happen to be able to assume a vaguely human form. The wolfish instincts are still very strong within her and often in conflict with her reason. She can rationalize what she did in her mind but never in her heart, and you played a dangerous game with that balance."

Odhinn rose and stood leaning on his spear, looking down at the Valkyrie. "By rights I should send you on your way and handle this matter myself. I am willing to give you a second chance, on the assumption that you have learned something from this. But, from this time on, you are to comply with my orders scrupulously, and never strike out on some plan of your own without first consulting me."

* * *

Signy slipped through the forest as quickly and quietly as she could. The night was still young, but she hoped to be well away from this place before it got much older. Every person, every warrior, maid or drudge in Siggier's hall lay asleep from the effects of her wand. Then, for good measure, she had done the same in the barracks and to the guards along the pier. Her remaining concern was for the special guards, the dark elves and landvaetir. She could take any that she found, but she did fear arrows out of the dark. But she did wish a slow and painful death on that disgusting weasel, and almost hoped to happen upon him in the woods.

She followed the game-trail down from the northeast, a very round-about way, but the only one she could follow in the dark, for the moon had not yet risen, and she had missed the lesser path. Unfortunately, this also placed her on the wrong side of the stream. She was picking her way carefully over the water-worn rocks, a series of falls shaped like four massive steps strewn with boulders, trying to find a place where she could jump the broad stream without wetting her fur. A black shape suddenly rose up over the top of a large, flat boulder not ten paces away. She could not see what it was, beyond a long neck, upstanding ears and two gleaming eyes. Then the head lifted higher, as if in surprise, and the ears twitched.

"Signy, is that you?" Sigmund asked, and rose to stand on top of the boulder.

"Sigmund?" Signy lifted her head and unhaunched her shoulders, then leaped to the top of the rock to join him. She put her mouth to his before he could protest; wolves, graced with long, slender snouts, were most passionate and involving at the acquired art of kissing.

"Did everything go well?" Sigmund asked.

Signy nodded. "All is ready. There is not a person awake in the entire hall. We can get the sword, take what we need, and be well out to sea before anyone will awaken.''

"Then we go . . . ?''

"As soon as the moon rises," she promised. "There are landvaetir and who knows what else running about.''

"Wolves!" Sigmund said ominously.

"I trust not," Signy replied. "None of Siggier's type, at least.''

She rose and stood for a moment, facing east. The forest was open over the stream for some distance in that direction, and she could see nearly to the eastern horizon. A pale golden glow against the night sky suggested that the moon would not be long in rising, perhaps no more than a few minutes. She sat back on her haunches and sighed heavily. Sigmund sat down close beside her and rubbed his muzzle gently against her own.

"Soon, now," she said. "Soon we will be free.''

"Yes, free," Sigmund agreed. "It seems to me like forever since this began, and yet less than four weeks have passed since my capture. My last free act was an attempt to break the sword and spare us this fate. I forget that the last ten years have been like living in a cage for you.''

"A cage," Signy repeated, leaning her head against his neck. "Yes, a wolf in a cage, tamed by my master for all to see and marvel at the deed. Never beaten. Never starved. And yet the torment I have endured was as bitter as any physical torture. There were lies and bitter words from the first, every heart and mind turned against me with no hope of finding a friend to comfort me. In those days he made me wait upon his will and serve him at the table like a drudge. When my children were born human, he took them away from me within the hour and spread the rumor that I would have devoured them because they were not born wolves. And so I did destroy them in the end.''

She paused, frowning in bitter remembrance, and Sigmund could think of no soothing words. But after a moment she settled her shoulder against his, finding more comfort in that than in anything he might have said.

"I began to miss the little things that I had lost, the woods and the wind and running on four legs, until that became a torment in itself. But most of all I missed you. We were always meant to belong to each other. But the cage is open now, for you have come for me. All that I have suffered, all the shame and disgrace that I have had to endure in painful silence, all that I have wished and wept for will be answered this night."

"This night you will have your answer, but of your own making," Sigmund told her gently. "I was caught and thrown into a cage of my own. You fought to free us both."

"I am not a beast to be captured and tamed," Signy said fiercely. "He forgot that I entered the cage by my own will, and that it was not for him that I submitted myself to be tamed."

Worried, Sigmund nuzzled her gently. "Do not torment yourself with painful memories. You have endured torment enough. The darkness lies behind you now, and brighter days are ahead."

Signy nodded absently. "Yes, that is so. It has been like a long, dark winter that would never end. But the winter is past at last, and I am returning to the springtime of life. The sun shines bright and warm by day, and moon and stars at night. And as much as I thought I missed such things, I never realized how much until now. You have brought it for me."

Sigmund smiled. "I could not bring you the spring, because it was never gone. Did you never look out your window toward the woods and see it waiting for you? The storms of winter have been gone these many months, giving way to light and hope and the reawakening of the fullness of life. Feel the gentle breeze that winds through wood and meadow, stirring leaf and grass. Catch the elusive scent it bears like messages through the night, telling of the sharp freshness of pine and the deep richness of the earth. These are the things that speak to you of home, of feelings of belonging, contentment and delight. The wilderness knows that you have returned where you belong, and it welcomes and reassures you with familiar delights."

"And yet it could never be home to me, not without you," she told him softly. "All the happiness the wilderness can promise is incomplete without your love."

Sigmund smiled and nuzzled her gently, then took up her mouth in his a second time, a short, reassuring kiss that quickly became one of deeper passion and commitment. At that same instant the moon rose far in the east, bathing the pair in golden radiance that grew and strengthened with each passing moment. So they sat in the gentle light for what seemed like a very long time before parting at last. Signy rubbed the side of her head in the deep fur of his neck, and they both looked up at the rising moon.

"There she sits, like a nosy old woman peering at us through the bushes," Signy said, smiling in tolerant amusement. "And yet I welcome her intrusion. I feel as though she has looked down upon us here and blessed our union with her gift of fragile beauty. She lights our hall on our wedding night, as close to a proper wedding as we will likely ever have. I wish that we might keep this magical moment forever."

Sigmund smiled. "There must surely be some magic in the air this night. Here we are, two foolish wolves alone in this big world. And we sit here beneath the moon and the stars and say such fine things as if we did not have a care in the world. Let us finish our task and be on our way from this place, and all the days to come will be ours."

Signy laughed and jumped down, crossing the stream in three quick leaps, then took off at a full run down the shorter path leading to Siggier's hall. Startled by the suddenness of her flight, Sigmund followed quickly, trying to make up for his lost time. They were as nearly equal in build as twins of the opposite sex could be, more so in their true forms, but he reasoned that his sister was out of shape from ten years of sitting beside the hearth. But he was mistaken in that. She had waited for him, but she did not intend to be passed.

But she stopped short when she came to the edge of the woods, then flitted from shadow to shadow as she made her way to the main door. There she paused once again to shift back to her mortal form, for she had need of hands. She had paused that night to dress in her Volsung clothes, undoubtedly brought with her ten years before. The pants and tunic were faded and threadbare, the seams threatening to fail. Her boots were long since gone. Sigmund's clothes were hardly in better shape from his days in captivity. In one form or another, they would soon be living naked until they found time to make more.

Signy pulled open the door and entered the main hall with Sigmund not far behind. What he saw surprised him. There were small, bright fires in each of the two hearths, lamps were lit and a third of the trestle tables were laid out, and about sixty people lay sound asleep. Most had been seated at the table and had fallen forward on the boards, although many had tumbled backwards off their benches, a few no doubt cracking their skulls in the process. Servants had laid down their trays before falling asleep, although two had dropped their burdens.

But most startling to Sigmund was the fact that a live tree dominated the center of the vast room. That had been the first thing he had noticed, and as his gaze traveled back to it he saw that a sword had been driven up to its hilt in the center of the trunk. He took a few halting steps toward it and saw that it was indeed the weapon that he had carried for ten years. The belt and scabbard that had been made for it sat propped against the trunk immediately below. There was no doubt in his mind that the sword had been left for him; his only doubt was whether or not he wanted it back.

"Go on," Signy insisted. "The Wanderer meant for you to have it, and this time you must learn to use it as he intended. The sword has the power to free us from any fear."

Sigmund stepped up to the tree and lightly laid his hands on the hilt. He took a deep breath and pulled back, and the sword slipped loose so easily that he fell back a step before he caught himself. For a moment the blade seemed to be a length of raw lightning, flaring with light and magic. The hall fell into sudden darkness, and doors and shutters were thrown open as errant winds seemed to chase in and out. Then the spectacular display faded away quickly, and he held down the sword to look at it.

"The sword welcomes you," Signy said, looking both startled and delighted. "That was its promise that it can and will protect us, a demonstration of the power that could be at your command if you can learn how to use it. And this time you will. Now you stand guard here while I collect our provisions."

She hurried into the back portions of the hall. Sigmund slipped the sword into its sheath and glanced around, wishing that he had a bow instead. Without its powers, the sword was no better than an ordinary one. It was by no means his best weapon, while the bow was. He wished that he had asked Signy to find one; he could not go looking, and all of Siggier's household guards carried shields and long spears.

Then it occurred to him that Siggier was in this hall, in

this very room, and quite helpless. The man who had
dared to defy the gods and had attempted to destroy the
Volsungs, who would sell his own world to the Jotnar so
that he could rule the northlands in the name of the Lord of
Utgardh. The man who had caged and tormented Signy for
ten years like a wild animal he could not tame. And who
had sent the wolf of Jotunheim to the sons of Sigi as they
slept under his spell. It was fitting that the wolf of the
Vargarbraut should visit him while he slept under his own
spell, like fate repaying his deeds in kind.

Sigmund turned and started toward the main table, suspecting that the large figure slumped over on the boards at
its head was that of the Lord of Hafvang. His head was
stretched out on the table, his arms at his side, an invit-
ingly easy target. Sigmund drew the sword, flashing brightly
as it was unsheathed. His eyes were drawn to the sword,
and he paused, looking down at it. Why should he hesitate? Siggier deserved death, and a world would be saved
by his destruction. It would both avenge the Volsungs and
assure that the pitiful remnant of their race had a chance to
survive and thrive. They might even someday be free to
return to the Vargarbraut.

But not this way. Sigmund could accept the role of
executioner, but this would be murder, and he could never
accept that. Siggier was a murderer and took pleasure in
the deed, whether by stealth or at his leisure. Sigmund was
a Volsung, a wolf. He might take the appearance of something nearly human in form, but he did not want to imitate
the evil in that race. His kind had suffered too many evils
to ever accept such evil in themselves. Sigmund returned
his sword to its sheath. For good or ill, he had made his
decision.

Signy returned quickly, a large cloth sack, bulging with
provisions, over each shoulder. She also carried bows
hung by their strings about her neck and bundles of ar-

rows, as many as she could manage, under each arm. They were not the light bows such as the Volsungs favored, which they had first acquired from the elves, but the larger bows of Siggier's warriors. Sigmund ran to her to retrieve his share of the burden.

"Bows!" he exclaimed in delight. "Oh, bless you, sister of mine! That is exactly what I wanted."

"Give me credit for arranging matters better than that," she said. "Come! I don't want to waste another moment of my life in this place!"

Bows in hand, they slipped cautiously into the darkness. They hurried down to the piers and quickly found a ship small enough for them to manage but large enough to trust to the open sea, and Sigmund made it ready to sail while his twin threw torches in all of Siggier's great warships. And so it was that they left Siggier's great fleet in flames.

CHAPTER ELEVEN

The little ship followed the brisk evening wind that carried it along the curve of the shore and finally out of the mouth of the bay. It turned northward along the coast, angling out somewhat toward open water. The single sail was brought around to take advantage of the wind that now caught the small vessel mostly from the side. Few other ships would have been able to take advantage of that wind, and would have been left helpless but for oars. The presence of a centerboard helped it to turn a wind from the side into forward motion. Wolfling ships, bound to and from their secret hall in the far north, had evaded pirate ships before by sailing in a direction ordinary ships could not follow. But that trick would not help them much should one of Siggier's warships find them.

Two figures stood, watching patiently, from the high cliffs overlooking the north shore of the bay's mouth. Golden moonlight glinted from the armor of the smaller watcher, standing unconcerned on a tiny out-thrust tongue of rock. The dark, towering figure of a man stood nearby, wrapped in the flowing folds of a black robe like a threatening storm against the clear night sky, leaning upon a long spear. A pair of horses also waited, well back from the ledge, chatting sociably to pass the time.

"Well, they are safely away at last," Odhinn said as he pulled off his hat and started back to where Sleipnir stood. "I was beginning to wonder if they were going to be all night about it."

Brynhild stared at him in surprise, wondering if something did not please him. "The Volsungs are very capable."

"Capable of getting themselves into more trouble than the two of us can save them from," Odhinn said as he folded away his robe. "They are bewildering, impulsive and sentimental to a fault. And so are you, my dear. Some day you will get yourself in trouble, following your heart instead of your head."

"I already have," she reminded him.

"I trust that you have learned your lesson better than the wolflings have," he answered and shook his head in resignation. "Where did I go wrong? It must have been trying to fit an intelligent mind into a canine skull."

"But what is wrong with them?" the Valkyrie asked, mystified. "Signy never missed a clue I left her, and she did figure out for herself that she could transfer through solids in the act of shape-changing."

Odhinn turned and looked at her in surprise. "Did she? It took Idhunn tens of thousands of years to catch the significance of that."

"Well, I certainly did not tell her," Brynhild insisted. "I did not even know it, since I don't have the power of shape-changing. And she is very good at figuring things out. Given her limited knowledge of what is going on, she came to some very logical conclusions."

"If wrong. Perhaps I should send her after Fafnir, rather than her brother. His only chance of catching Fafnir would be if he could sneak up behind him while the foolish dragon is brushing his teeth!" Odhinn declared scornfully, throwing up his hands. Then he saw Brynhild watching him closely and paused. "You would be in favor of that?"

"Under the circumstances, yes. Sigmund fears magic too much to ever command the sword fully, while Signy would never tire of probing its secrets. She is a match for her brother in speed, skill and strength, and there is no question that she exceeds him in wit and imagination. And, perhaps, even courage. It might be best that the sword should pass to her. She would get you the ring."

"She is also smart enough to learn its secrets in short order," Odhinn added. "And smart enough to prevent me from getting it away from her."

"Signy's loyalty is beyond question," Brynhild countered. "If the Wanderer asked, then she would surrender it without question."

"What are we arguing about?" Odhinn demanded suddenly. "Valkyrie, what are you trying to sell me?"

She looked at him questioningly. "What is your complaint with the Volsungs?"

Odhinn caught himself, mouth open, on the verge of a hot retort. His expression became thoughtful as he crossed his arms and leaned back against Sleipnir's massive shoulder. Both the horse and the Valkyrie watched him expectantly, but he stood deep in thought for a long moment, considering something with extreme care. At last he glanced over at Brynhild, watching her closely in a way that let her know she would soon be very useful to his plans.

"How would you like for one of the other Valkyries to take your patrol for a few weeks . . . or a few years?" he asked, as if offering her a favor.

"I would not like it," Brynhild admitted frankly. "I take it that you would have me doing something else for that time?"

"I would like for you to watch the Volsungs very closely, all the time," he explained. "As closely as possible. In fact, I would like for you to become a Volsung."

"Is that so?" Brynhild needed only a moment to figure out his plans. "Can you guide the shape-changing?"

Odhinn nodded. "I can make you appear to be a Volsung in every way, not by illusion but in truth. I will even give them false memories of you from the time before Siggier's attack. And I already have an excuse for your sudden and most opportune appearance that even Signy will not question."

"And what if they decide that I should aid in the noble cause of perpetuating the species?"

Odhinn grinned mischievously. "In your case, it would be perpetrating the species. As deftly as you've handled them up until now, you should be able to guide their thoughts away from the practicality of that suggestion. However, while the shape-changing is in effect, you will be a true wolfling, and any children you may have. . . ."

"There are limits to the devotion of even your most loyal Valkyrie."

"Now, would I seriously ask such a thing of you? Valkyries were not meant for motherhood."

"One more question. What if they ask me to become a wolf?"

"That is no problem," Odhinn assured her. "While you might not be a shape-changer yourself, I can give you the form of a functional shape-changer."

"That sounds like a paradox," the Valkyrie remarked testily.

"Of course it does, so don't think about it."

Night was beginning to fall by the time that Brynhild could clearly see the small ship that was coming directly toward her. She sat down to wait. She was uncomfortable, not just with the temporary form that Odhinn had given her but with the strange elvish dress. She missed her armor more than she had anticipated. The shape-changing had taken several inches from her former height and a third of her weight; she had been tall and rangy, but now she was small and delicate. Her mane tickled and itched inside her shirt, and she was occasionally disconcerted when her pointed ears lifted and twitched of their own accord. Her one consolation was that wearing her wolf form was even more uncomfortable; she hoped that she would never be expected to run something down and catch it.

She found, much to her own surprise, that she was actually very apprehensive about this meeting. For the first time in her life she was confronted by questions that she had never considered. Her mind turned again and again to Odhinn's teasing suggestion that she should have Sigmund mate with her. Odhinn had long been the only mate she had ever wanted, even if their relationship was never physical but always formal and distant. She was led to wonder if somewhere, or at some time yet to come, there might be a true mate that she could welcome and cherish. And if she might have a child. The thought of a Valkyrie daughter had never occurred to her. But a wolfling daughter, small, swift and free . . . such a thought did stir her interest.

Perhaps, ultimately, she did have cause to fear this meeting. This chance to be a Volsung for a time came as an open invitation to indulge herself in new thoughts and experiences, even a new life. Sigmund would be expected to mate with her, and she already knew that she would find it hard to refuse . . . that she would not. And she feared that, when their duties were done and the wolflings departed for the elf-world, she might go with them, remain what she had become, rather than return to her old duties. She feared it because she also wanted it.

"Very soon now," Glaerfaxi said under her breath.

Brynhild looked up. The Volsungs were giving up their hopeless tack against a headwind, dropping their sail and bringing up the centerboard. Then they broke out oars to row the final hundred yards to shore.

Fortunately, Odhinn himself had taken the final important step, placing in their minds the memory of a wolfling named Brynhild. If all went well, they would remember her as a childhood companion, a few years younger than themselves and so not a close acquaintance. Sigmund knew even more about her, or who she was supposed to be, than his sister. She knew, of course, all there was to know about them, as prominent members of her pack. Otherwise she was to sight, touch and smell a wolfling, and wolflings had only one origin. She could even become a wolf to prove her claim.

She rose and walked down the beach to the edge of the water, stepping gingerly over wave-worn stones. Few wolflings, especially younger ones, ever wore shoes, and her lack of boots, any weapon but her spear, and her general appearance would support her story. Her clothes were worn and smelled of smoke, one sleeve scorched as if in the fires from Siggier's catapults.

"Stop stumbling around," Glaerfaxi hissed under her breath. "You are going to give yourself away."

"It hurts!" Brynhild hissed back.

"Then you can appreciate the value of horses," Glaerfaxi said smugly. "We go through life with our shoes nailed on."

"Be quiet!" Brynhild said sternly. Volsung hearing was even more sharp than smell.

The little ship glided in with surprising speed for having only two of its ten oars out. The wolflings brought their oars in quickly to allow the ship to drift for the last few yards, bracing themselves as it slid a fourth of its length up onto the beach, so close to where the Valkyrie stood that she had to leap out of the way. Sigmund threw her a line that she ran up the beach to tie to the rock where she had been sitting.

By the time that she had turned back, the two wolflings had jumped down from the ship and stood staring, not so much at her but at Glaerfaxi. Wolflings had little love for horses, and horses had none for wolflings. Moreover, Glaerfaxi was of the children of Sleipnir, immense by the standards of mortal breeds, perfect in form. Her saddle and halter were trimmed in silver, and she obviously held no bit. A Volsung's association with such a horse was no doubt puzzling to them.

"Your horse?" Signy asked.

"My companion," Brynhild answered.

Sigmund glanced at her now and started. "Brynhild?"

She nodded, privately relieved that the false memories had so quickly come to play.

"You know her?" Signy asked.

"Of course. She must have been very young when you went away. This is Brynhild."

"Brynhild, daughter of Ranari and Regvan, of the line of Rannvieg," she introduced herself. "And I do not have to ask that you are Signy. You have not changed since the morning you left us."

"But you have," Sigmund said and turned to his sister. "She must have been only seven or eight when you departed, all mane and long legs. Father was going to arrange her mating with Kari . . . ah, sort of formal recognition of what they had been doing in the woods for the past year. Kari is dead, I fear."

Brynhild caught herself quickly and hoped that her incredulous expression had been mistaken for surprise at that news. She had been unprepared for that, a most unsubtle joke on Odhinn's part, laid like a trap in the unsuspecting Volsung's memory. She glanced at Glaerfaxi. The horse's tight-set mouth was trembling, and her eyes glittered with silent laughter.

"I have been told of that before," she said. "But that is a long story. I have prepared wood for a fire, at the edge of the forest out of the wind, and shelter for the night. If you can provide food, then I will tell you that story over dinner."

The two Volsungs were very agreeable, their hunger and exhaustion now almost as great as their curiosity. Brynhild had a warm blaze burning before the other two returned from the ship with provisions.

"It happened that Sigi was leading the remaining Volsungs west and somewhat north following Siggier's attack," Brynhild explained over dinner while the twins listened attentively. "He knew where the place was that we could cross into the elf-world, and he trusted that we would be allowed to pass. He really had no other choice, since we could not get to the ships."

"The Wanderer said that they would be allowed to pass," Signy reported.

"On the second day I dropped far back behind the rest to scout," Brynhild continued. "I fell and broke a foreleg, so that I could no longer run as a wolf. And I could not catch up with the rest, not in human form, without food or water or even boots. I followed as best I could for many days, but I did not know where I was going or how I would even know if I was there.

"But last night the Wanderer came to me. He mended my broken arm with a touch. He said that I must go to Vikfjallaland, to meet you here, and that I must help you in any way that I can. He said that the great horse Glaerfaxi would bring me here and then stay with me, to offer what help she can."

"She brought you here since last night?" Sigmund asked.

"But you must have been in the lands far to the east of the Hronn."

Brynhild nodded.

"So I was, but she brought me here with time to spare. She flew!" the Valkyrie added with what she hoped was the proper degree of awe and excitement.

The two Volsungs glanced over at Glaerfaxi, who was trying hard not to laugh.

"But I do not understand," Sigmund protested. "What can a horse do?"

"Well, for one thing, she talks."

"She does?"

"Of course I do," Glaerfaxi answered for herself. "And I will gladly do what I can for you, but please do not ask more of me than you have been told. I am a steed such as the Valkyries ride, a daughter of Sleipnir. I fly. I speak. My strength is great, and I have other small powers."

"She has told you no more?" Signy asked.

"The only thing I have established from our conversation is that she thinks I smell as bad as I believe her to," Brynhild replied, then looked to Sigmund. "I hardly need to ask, but do you plan to settle in the northern hall of the Volsungs?"

"That is our intention," he replied. "Siggier does not know of our northern holding. No one does, as far as I am aware. We intend that it should remain that way."

"And you have the magic sword given to you by the Wanderer?"

"I have it."

"Then I would say that we are as well off as we can be," she said, deciding that she had elaborated on her story sufficiently to explain her presence. Glaerfaxi's presence was the part that she considered the hardest to explain, for the Volsungs had little use for a talking, flying horse and there was certainly no empathy between the two species. But there had been no leaving the horse behind, for Glaerfaxi was not just her steed but her counterpart.

"Kari spoke often of you, those days that we were held captive," Sigmund said as he poked at the fire with a stick. Either his false memories were extensive, or he had made use of a polite lie to reassure her.

"Kari is not gone," she said in return. "The Wanderer told me that all of the Volsungs who have died have been restored to life and returned to the others in the elf-world. They cannot return to us now, not after passing from this realm, but they are well and safe."

"Is that so? I might almost forgive the Wanderer for his meddling," Sigmund said, but he was grateful enough for that news. But even Brynhild thought it small compensation for what his kind had endured.

Brynhild stood guard over the ship, shivering discreetly in the chill air of dawn. Her nose was cold, her big, pointed ears were cold, and especially her poor feet. The two wolflings, of course, did not have the grace to be cold. Therefore, she was doubly cursed with the task of pretending not to notice that she was miserable, not just to maintain appearances but to protect her pride. Valkyries were supposed to be hearty, but all she could think of was how much she missed her padded armor.

The night tide had left the ship well up on the beach, so that Glaerfaxi's strength was needed to slide it back out. Now it floated free, only a small portion of its keel resting in the sand, and Brynhild was kept busy trying to prevent the wind and waves from turning the ship sideways to the shore.

The wolflings were attending to their morning duties at the edge of woods. Brynhild was surprised to see that they did not even bother to drop their pants, for they simply converted to wolf form. Otherwise they were as indiscreet as animals; she found it interesting to note that they possessed a curious double standard of morality, unhesitantly allowing behavior in wolf form that they would never consider otherwise. Unfortunately, that only complicated her own position.

She turned to Glaerfaxi, who stood a few paces away watching her activities with droll amusement. She was beginning to wish that she had insisted that Glaerfaxi remain in Asgardh, for the aggravating horse obviously viewed the whole affair as a grand joke, the humbling of a once-great Valkyrie.

"Perhaps you should go ahead and get in the boat," Brynhild suggested.

Glaerfaxi lowered her head to regard the ship, then looked back at Brynhild. "I don't think that I want to get in that boat. I'll fly."

"It would look suspicious to have you flying overhead."

"Three wolflings and a horse in a boat does not look suspicious? And what if the waves cause me to loose my balance? If I fall on one of you, that would be the end. It would be best that I fly."

Brynhild nodded and fell silent, tending the ship until the Volsungs came to release her from her watch. She paced quickly up the beach and disappeared into the forest. Sigmund proceeded to toss their provisions and equipment into the ship, but Signy stood and watched the Valkyrie until she was hidden from view by brush and shadow. After a moment she turned to her brother.

"How well do you know that girl?" she asked softly. "What do you think of her?"

"Brynhild?" Sigmund asked, mildly surprised. "Why, I have known her all my life. She seems capable enough."

"I do not remember her at all," Signy remarked.

"How many others do you not remember? Of course, I never really saw much of her until she took up with Kari, but I always approved that match. She reminds me of you in small ways, cunning and cautious.'' He paused and stared at her. ''What are you suspicious of?''

''Everyone and everything, after all that we have been through,'' she replied and shrugged. ''She looks like a wolfling. She has to be a wolfling. And yet there are things about her. She has what might be a trace of an accent when she speaks elvish. But the words of the mortal language I heard her speak last night were perfect.''

''I find that unremarkable,'' Sigmund said frankly.

''She moves wrong,'' Signy insisted. ''Her walk is wrong. And the ground obviously hurts her, the way that humans can never walk quickly and unconcerned without their shoes.''

''That does not surprise me, since she has been walking in mortal form, ragged, half starved and without shoes for nearly four weeks. She is foot-sore and nearly exhausted.''

''Nor is she in any way frightened of that horse,'' Signy added, unconvinced. ''I know that I could never be on good terms with such a beast. Wolflings as a rule do not like horses.''

''But there are exceptions, and Brynhild is obviously one. She looks like a wolfling. She smells like a wolfling. And we have seen that she can become a wolf.''

''Of course.''

Sigmund caught the suspicious note in her voice and regarded her closely. ''Do you think that she is not the Brynhild that I remember?''

''Or the Brynhild you remember never existed,'' Signy said and shrugged again. ''Still, whatever she is, I do not doubt that she is only here to help us.''

CHAPTER TWELVE

By the time they reached the northern hall of the Volsungs, Brynhild was beginning to suspect that she was fooling no one but herself. Sigmund and Signy said nothing to openly question her authenticity as a wolfling, but they were subtly, unobtrusively helping her to learn exactly how a wolfling was supposed to behave. It was as if they were helping her to maintain her deception, quite in spite of herself. They appeared to accept that she had been sent to help and that she was supposed to be a wolfling, and they played the game without question.

The northern holding was far larger than it had been when abandoned by the Volsungs in the time of Rerir. Less than a hundred wolflings, mortals and cubs had lived in the three original halls while eight now stood, ready to accommodate over four hundred, built by the work teams that Sigmund had been leading there for the past eight summers. He was inclined to consider it a wasted effort. This holding, meant to accommodate his entire race, now awaited only himself, his sister and a strange girl whose presence he did not openly question. But if the effort meant that the three of them would be safe, then it had surely been worthwhile.

Sigmund pushed open the door of the main hall and

entered cautiously. He held aloft the sword and for once it obliged by glowing with a strong white radiance. Assuring that the place was empty was easy to determine, for the hall appeared untouched since he had closed the door nearly a year before. Everything had been made ready for several hundred Volsungs, cold, hungry, perhaps wounded and certainly traveling light. Everything they might need lay at hand, even to having wood laid out in every hearth with torches and lamps ready. A cloud of dust, undisturbed, indicated that the place had never been touched.

Signy entered without awaiting her brother's clearance, and the Valkyrie followed quickly, knowing that she was by far the most capable of the three to defend them. But the question of possible danger was quickly dismissed. She addressed herself to lighting a fire, a task that always befell her because the wolflings either thought that she was very good at it or knew she used magic. She had a blaze started in a matter of minutes and passed lighted lamps to the Volsungs, who immediately set off to check the other buildings. Glaerfaxi shambled in, uninvited. She poked her nose over Brynhild's shoulder, snorted ambiguously, and wandered off to check the provisions.

"So this is home," Signy said as she returned.

"So it would seem," Brynhild agreed as she began opening boxes in her search for something for dinner. "I suppose that there are no cattle?"

"No, of course not," Signy replied as she began to look through boxes. "What Sigmund planned for I don't know, except that there should be enough dried beef and venison, cheese and flour to feed several hundred wolflings for at least several weeks. That should last the three of us quite some time. Of course, if we want fresh, we will have to hunt."

"I found the cheese," Brynhild said, disquieted by the

thought of hunting. "What I want right now is fresh clothes."

"Sigmund will have to show us where things are . . . if he even remembers," Signy said, pausing in her task to pull off the ragged pants and tunic she wore. "Go ahead and take those off, if you want."

The Valkyrie's hands moved as if to cover herself, as though the worn clothes had been ripped from her. Signy saw the move and looked at her questioningly. "I was away for quite some time, but since when had Volsungs become prudish? Sigmund. . . ."

She paused with the startled look of someone who has remembered something she should not have forgotten, something decidedly impolitic. That left Brynhild to wonder what odd fact it could be. She also saw no alternative and quickly removed her own clothes.

"I would not steal your game," she said as she undressed, wondering if it was a proper wolfling analogy.

Signy only smiled. "My dear girl, there are in all Midhgardh two female wolflings and only one male. Our race has never been in such danger of extinction. Some arrangements will have to be made. Besides, taking off your clothes can imply putting on your fur."

Brynhild shrugged and poked at the fire; it was too late now, and she would have to get used to it sometime. Too many things the wolfling had said left her wondering if Signy either did or did not know that she was not a Volsung in truth, or if she simply had not yet decided. She was unnerved enough that Signy already had plans to mate her with Sigmund, something she supposedly would not do if she knew who the Valkyrie really was. Brynhild was seized with a growing desire to go home . . . and, to her alarm, a thrill of excitement.

• • •

Signy padded up the hillside as quietly as she could. The night was dark and very deep, so that every clattering pebble seemed to echo endlessly through the valleys and ridges of these mountains. Sigmund had come this way; she could not see him, but the gentle breeze carried his scent to her. The night was still new, and the light chill in the air made her feel young and full of life.

Sigmund suddenly stepped out before her just a few paces ahead, and she ran up to his side. He seemed so large and powerful beside her, for all she knew that they were almost exactly the same size, so warm and comforting, perhaps because she wanted to believe it so. He nuzzled her gently and smiled.

"Hello! What are you doing out?" he asked with teasing innocence.

"Just looking at the moon. Have you ever howled at the moon?"

"Howling?" Sigmund asked. "No. Not since I met you."

"I cannot believe that! I have given you no satisfaction."

"Would it be enough for me to say that I delight in anticipation?" he asked,.and chuckled. "What of Brynhild?"

"I left her in the main hall, poking through the supplies. She is terribly upset that you did not bring shoes along with all the other clothes."

"Am I supposed to think of everything?"

"I doubt that a pair of boots would solve her problem," Signy remarked, looking down at the hold in the valley below. "I am beginning to think that she has never walked in human form before."

"Then what is she?"

"A wolfling, of course. But one that the Wanderer has brought from the elf-world. One born of the wolflings who departed long ago. Of course, she is hardly used to wearing shoes or a hundred other things we take for granted."

Sigmund laughed. "Poor girl! But if she is so inept, then why was she sent?"

"To have children," Signy said, and smiled. "I suggested it to her, and it all but scared her to death. I get the feeling that the girl is older than I am, much older, and yet far less knowledgeable about the ways of the world. This world, at least."

"Do you honestly expect me to mate with this girl?"

"Yes, if she allows it. I, however, intend to press a prior claim."

Which did indeed appear to be her intention. She trotted off to one side of the path, to a place beneath the trees where the bed of pine needles was thick and soft. She lay down on one side, her long tail twitching alluringly with a cat-like movement. Sigmund approached cautiously and lay down close beside her.

"You do mean business, do you not?" he asked teasingly.

"I do. And this time I will accept no excuses."

"I hope that I will have to make no excuses."

She rubbed her muzzle against his, and they kissed long and passionately. Then Signy stretched out completely on her side, inviting him to come and lay close against her, and they shared their love in the wolfling manner.

Hardly a month passed before Sigmund and Signy left Brynhild to watch the holding while they made their way back down the long mountain slopes to their hidden ship. Glaerfaxi went along as guard. They were to sail far to the south to one of the trading villages and return with certain supplies they did not have, particularly cattle. It was a journey that should have taken a couple of weeks. But they returned after only a couple of days, running in wolf form as they herded the cattle between them, the horse bringing up the rear looking melancholy and slightly harassed. They had happened across a merchant traveler in the very bay where their ship was hidden and had made their purchases from him.

Their quick return came as a surprise to Brynhild, but she was far from pleased. She thought that the Volsungs had not been cautious enough, something she could hardly believe after all they had been through. They should have let this merchant go his own way, she insisted, and then continued on with their original plan. They had nowhere else to run, and Signy was now pregnant with a child she would have early the following spring, the time when all wolfling cubs were born. This only made Brynhild all the more apprehensive, and for more reasons than one. She had been indulging her own dreams, and now had to admit that she would soon be pregnant herself . . . if she was not already.

There was a minor celebration in Volsung Hall that night to honor the safe return of the travelers. It did not last long, however, for the travelers were tired from running herd on their cattle. Glaerfaxi claimed that she was not feeling her oats and quite literally went to sleep standing up. Sigmund teased Brynhild into another mating, supported by Signy's insistence that time was running short that year, and the Valkyrie acquiesced in spite of herself. Soon Sigmund retired with his own mate to their room, finding Brynhild to be in too foul a mood to remain with her that night, and she cried herself to sleep. That too was a very new experience for a very old Valkyrie.

Brynhild woke suddenly late in the night. She could not at first guess what might have disturbed her, but then she heard the odd bellows of the cattle and sensed their rising terror. So used was she becoming to wolfling form and ways that she did not even consider pausing to dress but hurried to the main door. Once outside she shifted form and trotted off toward the barn.

There was enough moon for her keen eyes to pierce the darkness easily, and she immediately saw that the barn

door stood partly open. That suggested pirates, or someone, come to raid the livestock, and she first suspected that
the wolflings had been followed. But, as she approached
the door cautiously, the only scent she caught was not
mortal but animal. Bear, her nose suggested uncertainly,
since it was an animal that she had never before encountered. Bears were very bright, she reasoned, and therefore
cautious. An angry, determined wolf, especially one half
again normal size, should be enough to drive it away. She
put on her best snarl, growling deep in her throat, and
marched inside the open door.

Her mistake was immediately obvious. The bear was
angrier and even more determined and a great deal larger
still. She went in looking for the beast, only to have it
come out of the shadows behind her, forcing her to retreat
quickly into a corner. Only the fact that she was still quite
formidable saved her. She was able to keep the beast away
from her, but not force it to retreat far enough for her to
escape the corner. The battle quickly stalemated.

Brynhild saw only one good chance, and she took it.
Gathering her courage, she stood perfectly still, growling
deep in her throat with her head bent almost to the ground.
Instinct told her that this action would work, and so it did.
The bear dropped to all fours and ambled toward her,
grunting and growling in return. She leaped straight onto
the bear's back, gathered herself and leaped for the overhanging ledge of the loft. It was quite a jump, fifteen feet
out and twelve up, and just a little too much. She caught
the edge with her forelegs and hung dangling, unable to
draw herself up.

The bear turned and shuffled over to stand below her,
reaching up with its short, powerful arms. Brynhild was
able to save herself by drawing up her hind legs and tail,
furiously reviewing her favorite magic tricks for something
that might help. Instead she fell directly on the bear's

upturned head, sending them both rolling. The beast came up rolling and thrashing, and she barely managed to leap out of its grasp. She retreated back into the corner, exactly where she had started and now the worse for wear.

Sigmund appeared in the doorway at that moment. He paused only an instant to survey the situation, then raised the sword he carried, holding the hilt firmly in both hands, the point aimed at the bear. The blade pulsed once with light, and a dazzling bolt of raw energy shot from the tip. It passed unhindered through the bulk of the animal and on through the wooden planking of the wall, leaving a smoking hole. The bear hesitated in its attack, then fell heavily.

Sigmund lowered the sword and stepped into the barn, advancing to stand over the body of the bear. Signy followed closely, and Glaerfaxi stuck her head in the door but would not enter. She snorted in disgust at the thick, unpleasant smoke that filled the air, rather like one of Signy's early attempts at cooking. Sigmund prodded the bear with his sword to be certain, then looked over to where Brynhild sat in the corner, panting heavily from her exertions with her long tongue hanging out.

"You really should be more careful," he remarked. "Northern bears can be very dangerous."

Brynhild's reply to that was both simple and direct.

"Were you hurt?" Signy asked as she approached and began to inspect her fur for damage.

"Not me," Brynhild said. She converted back to mortal form and was slightly dismayed to find herself naked, but then so were they all. "And please do not hover over me like a pack of crows! I am neither hurt nor frightened, and only just a little aggravated. My suggestion is that we get this carcass out of the barn so that the cattle will shut up and go back to sleep, and us as well."

"Good idea," Sigmund agreed. "Let's find some ropes so that Glaerfaxi can drag it."

"Long ropes!" the horse declared.

"Oh, and congratulations on your command of the sword," Brynhild added. "It seems that you no longer need me to protect you."

By appearances, quite to the contrary, she thought, and that for a Valkyrie was most embarrassing. She might as well be pregnant.

Siggier seated himself with weary resignation, noticing the layer of dust on his plate. He wiped it away with his sleeve; the shirt was fresh and no doubt cleaner than any rag a servant would have brought. A necessary evil until the last of the tree could be removed, but he could no longer stand the sight of that tree. That naturally led him to other, less pleasant thoughts that he would rather not review over dinner, such as the reason why he had come to hate that tree. Why half of his grand fleet lay in charred ruin at the bottom of the bay. The reason for his private humiliation, and his loss of prestige among his people, especially his warriors.

His one guest for dinner was a weasel of a man, a transient merchant who had come bobbing in on a leaky knorr that morning. A weasel and a bore, who thought his petty ploys were of great import, making him something of an equal to the weaselly Lord of Hafvang. At least the man had been cautioned against asking embarrassing questions, such as why timber was being cut in the main hall, or where the Lady of the Holding was.

Siggier saw the man start, staring at someone halfway down the table. He looked and saw that it was only Trigin the weasel, taking his place with the rest of Siggier's lieutenants. He wondered if the merchant thought that he had found a long-lost cousin.

"Trigin, of Jotunheim," Siggier said blandly, amused. "He is my best tracker."

"That I do not doubt," the merchant said, as if going naturally into a sales routine. "Thought I knew what was true and what was legend, but there seems to be a surprise for me in every port."

"Oh?" Siggier prompted.

"Why, yes." The merchant stirred nervously, as if caught off guard. "Two or three weeks ago, as I was going down the coast of Vikfjallaland, we were laying out bad weather in a bay when out of the forest popped a pair of elves and the biggest damned horse I'd ever seen. Said they were setting up house back in the mountains. They wanted cattle and took five, as well as some bits I sold them. They did have gold and to spare!"

"Elves, you say?" Siggier asked, alert now and fearing danger to his realm. Vikfjallaland would be a big place to swallow, especially after his losses. But if elves were trying to settle there, eventually to move against him, then he must invade and hold that land against their intrusion.

"Yes, so they said. They certainly weren't mortal folk," the merchant said, but he sounded uncertain. "They had pointed ears and big eyes, and even the girl wore pants but they both walked barefoot. Of course, I had always heard that elves were tall and handsome. These folk were small and furry, brown as nuts with long gray hair. And they looked so alike that I could hardly tell them apart. Reminded me more of animals. They would look at you the way a fox or wolf might, if you caught it drinking at a stream."

"Did they have names?"

"None that they gave."

Siggier sat for a long moment in silence. Slowly he smiled, a smile of cold, murderous pleasure that filled those about him with fear. He turned to the merchant so swiftly that the man jumped. "Surely you could lead me to this place."

"I suppose I could," the merchant replied in a hesitant voice, fearful of suggesting that he wanted to know the profit of such a thing.

"I will make a bargain with you," Siggier continued. "Take me to this place, and I will give you back your life. If I find what I seek, then you will have a new ship. If I get what I desire, then I will fill that ship with treasure. Fair?"

"Infinitely!"

"Egil!" he called out, and the lieutenant approached quickly. "Egil, I am going to Vikfjallaland. I need a warship and warriors ready as soon as possible."

"It can be ready by dawn," Egil assured him. "May I ask why?"

Siggier smiled with grim satisfaction. "I'm going to hunt wolves."

Odhinn glanced up from his reading, setting the glowstones of his study to shine more brightly with a wave of his hand. Sigrune, still in her armor, stepped up to stand before him, standing at strict attention. She was always the most formal of the Valkyries, ordinarily an exuberant and easy-going lot, but he knew that something was wrong.

"Matters have taken an unexpected turn," she said. "Siggier knows of the general location of the Volsungs. He has a guide, a merchant, who sold his wares to the wolflings as they came out of hiding to buy cattle. He does not know their exact location, but he can cast about and make some logical deductions. . . ."

"And, possessing a truly amazing, devious genius, he will find them in a very short time," Odhinn finished for her. "But he has outsmarted himself. This time the Wanderer does not have to play games. Warn Brynhild. Tell her . . . no, wait."

He sat for a moment, deep in thought, before looking

up at the patient Valkyrie. "I think that I will go myself. This is an old debt that I must pay in person. Have Brynhild's armor bundled up and delivered to Sleipnir's stable."

"The armor will not fit," Sigrune pointed out.

"I will assist her back into her true form," Odhinn said coldly. "I do not know if Brynhild will be going back to the Volsungs. There will be no point now, and she is letting small matters get entirely out of hand."

Sigrune bowed her head and withdrew, hurrying off to complete her errand. Odhinn paused for a moment to consider the matter again, and decided that he was actually rather pleased with the way things were turning out. Siggier would soon be gone, his empire broken, and the Jotnar deprived of their ally. And he would be able to recall Brynhild before she slipped so far that she might defect into wolfling form forever. At that moment, the matter of Brynhild concerned him more than anything.

"You worry too much about the wrong things," a voice remarked from out of the very air.

Odhinn paused, commanding himself not to betray his alarm. She always played this game, savoring his dismay.

"Please do not put yourself to all of the trouble of paying me a visit," Jordh continued. "I am already here."

"So you are here," Odhinn replied. "Get to the point."

"I allowed you to keep your Volsungs in Midhgardh," Jordh began, quick and stern. "I could not believe that you would be so foolish as to try and use them, but I still expected it. First you gave Sigmund a weapon that should never have been placed in less capable hands. Then the two Volsungs manage to settle near Fafnir's den, and you send a Valkyrie to protect them. Now you plan to go yourself to fight their battles for them."

"And what concern is that of yours? I only want to protect my Volsungs from dangers that are too great for them. I have already withdrawn most of them to the elf-world.''

''All of them should have gone.''

''If that is what you wish.''

''No, that is what you should have done. Now it is too late.''

''I do not want them harmed,'' Odhinn said, wondering what this was going to cost him. Waiting for the ax to fall, as the mortals said, but on the necks of the two Volsungs rather than his own.

''You may have them back, although in the manner that you recovered their brothers and so many others . . . if that is their fate,'' Jordh said. ''You were not so worried about protecting them, so long as you could re-animate their spirits. If that is a proper concern, then so shall it be with Sigmund and Signy.''

''If that is their fate?'' Odhinn asked.

''The wolflings must fight for themselves,'' she explained. ''They may fight or they may flee. If they can manage to keep themselves alive, then their lives are surely their own. But they must receive no help from you.''

''So it shall be,'' Odhinn reluctantly agreed. ''Sigmund can now make the sword serve him, as you are no doubt aware. His use of it undoubtedly awoke you. He might get all the help he needs from it.''

''I do not sleep,'' Jordh replied impatiently. ''Indeed, I have been watching this matter unfold for quite some time, and I have found it quite entertaining. But I never sleep.''

''So you have told me.''

''My last condition concerns the Valkyrie Brynhild,'' she continued. ''She has mated with Sigmund and conceived a child. That pregnancy must be terminated immediately.''

''That, in all fairness, I cannot allow!'' Although this news surprised and profoundly shocked him, Odhinn had the presence of mind to protest.

"You do not fool me!" Jordh declared. "Lord of Asgardh, I do see how your mind works, that you foresee a new race of wolflings who possess the powers of Valkyries. I cannot allow that."

Odhinn did not reply at once. What he had heard left him so shocked that he could barely speak. The thought of wolfling wizards had never occurred to him. All he knew was a deep sense of loss and betrayal. In truth, he did love Brynhild, and her alone. He had long been resigned to the fact that he could not know her sexually, and he preferred matters as they stood. She had never hinted that she wanted a mating. Now she was pregnant by a shape-changing wolf, and by her own choice.

"I do insist," Jordh prompted in his continued silence. "End that pregnancy, or I will destroy Brynhild myself."

"It shall be done," he agreed at last, although he did not want that child born himself.

"It shall be done," Jordh agreed. "And if you obey my terms, then I shall grant you this. If the wolflings are able to save themselves, either in flight or in battle, then you may return and lead them to the elf-world. Either way, once this matter is resolved, there will be no more Volsungs left alive in Midhgardh."

Odhinn looked up in the direction from which her voice came. "If that is all you want, then why will you not allow me to take them now?"

"Would you tolerate my suggestion that I wish to teach you a lesson?" Jordh asked. "Just as well, since I consider it impossible to teach you anything in the first place. Say then that I do not want the wolflings conveniently lost in the transfer, as has happened before. I would prefer that they die; you would still have them back, but they would be unable to return to my realm. Here comes Sigrune. Tell her to order Brynhild to return. Tell her that she cannot say why."

With that she was gone.

CHAPTER THIRTEEN

B rynhild unwrapped Glaerfaxi's saddle and gear and began to lay out the various pieces where she could find them. Dawn was only just in the air, and it was still so dark that she could not see what each piece was until she brought it out of the wooden box that Sigmund had given her for it nearly three months earlier. Glaerfaxi stood peering over her shoulder, blowing distracting clouds of steam in the cold morning air.

She struggled to hold back her tears as she worked, tears she certainly did not want the horse to see, since she did not understand them herself. The summons had been short and plain. No explanation had been given, although she could well suspect that she was in trouble. That did not bother her so much. The problem was that now was the time for her to decide, and she knew that she did not want to leave but had every desire to remain both what and where she was. And now it seemed that the choice was not even hers to make. The freedom as well as the happiness she thought she had was all an illusion, and that was bitterly disappointing.

"Brynhild?" Sigmund asked, suddenly behind her. Glaerfaxi was so startled that the Valkyrie had to jump back to keep from getting stepped on.

"What are you doing here?" she asked accusingly.

"Should I not be the one to ask you that?" Sigmund inquired in return. "Do you have to go?"

"The Wanderer has ordered it in no uncertain terms," Brynhild said as she began to saddle her horse.

"Why?" Sigmund asked as he helped lift the saddle into place.

"That I do not know. Perhaps you no longer need me. You are obviously able to command the sword. Perhaps I am in trouble for my disobedience." Sigmund looked so skeptical that she had to explain. "I was sent to protect you, not to mate with you. The Allfather wants the two of you to reestablish the Volsung race, and it seems that I am not to contribute in that respect."

"What would be wrong with your children?" Sigmund asked.

Brynhild paused. What indeed, unless they should inherit their mother's powers? This was the first time the possibility had occurred to her, and that thought also reminded her of the Fenris wolf. Perhaps there was more logic to the summons than she had anticipated. She continued her work without answering.

"And you were not going to tell us?" Signy asked, arriving at that moment. "Brynhild, what are we going to do without you?"

"You two have each other," Brynhild replied. "I do not even have that much. The question in my mind is what am I going to do without you."

"You may find a mate of your own now," Sigmund suggested.

Brynhild shook her head. "I want a wolfling mate. I want to remain a wolfling myself. It cannot be."

"Please, what are you?" Signy asked fearfully. "Who are you?"

"My name is Brynhild," she said, and paused, wondering how much she might say. "I am in reality a Valkyrie. I have protected the Volsungs from their earliest days. I hope that you can forgive me for not doing better."

The wolflings looked so surprised that she had to laugh. "You knew from the first that something was up. How do you think that I came by a Valkyrie's flying horse? The Allfather does not distribute them to just anyone."

"Well, thanks!" Glaerfaxi said, certain that she had been complimented grandly.

"Your memories, of course, are false," she continued. "I never knew Kari, much less mated with him. You are the only mate that I have ever known."

"But, why?" Sigmund asked as she pulled herself into the saddle.

Brynhild looked down at him with an uncertain smile. "I must have wanted to, I suppose, for I certainly could have stopped it. Perhaps because I wanted to stay a wolfling forever and looked upon it as an excuse. I have indulged my delusions, but it was not to be. Fate may be blind, but she remains a terrible mistress."

"Will we see you again?" Signy asked.

"I will be watching over you," she replied vaguely. "I must leave you now, for I do not know how to say farewell gracefully, and I certainly am not going to allow you to see a Valkyrie cry. Foxy, take us home!"

Glaerfaxi leaped into the air and disappeared, wrapping herself in the veil of illusion that allowed Valkyries to pass unseen. But she could not so easily make the Volsungs disappear from Brynhild's sight, so she allowed her great speed to carry them away as quickly as she could.

"So, you have seen fit to return to me," Odhinn said, glancing up from his papers to glare at her.

Brynhild, standing in the doorway of his study, had to fight an impulse to run and hide. She was very conscious

of her appearance, small and shaggy, dressed in simple
wood-elf's clothes and barefoot. Her wolfling form now
seemed to her an accusation of her defiance. She needed
him to return her to her true form, and yet that was the last
thing she desired.

"I will not presume to think that you might have taken
your duty too seriously," he continued. "I do remember
teasing you about it, but I also recall telling you to do what
you needed to avoid it. I will allow that you like being a
wolfling so much that you began to forget everything you
ever were."

"I was happy and free," Brynhild said, hesitantly defi-
ant. "Free to seek a future of my own. I never had those
things as a Valkyrie."

"Free to indulge in sex with a wolf?" Odhinn asked.

"He offered me more than you ever did."

"My duties would not allow it," Odhinn answered, but
gently. "Perhaps the Volsung do enjoy greater freedom
than I have ever known. Of course, I could hardly have
suggested such a thing to one of the iron maidens, the
chaste Valkyries of Asgardh. How was I to know that such
was your desire? If you had come to me, something could
have been arranged. Did you, in truth, actually ever desire
it?"

Brynhild considered, and shook her head. "No, I was
never free to even consider it. As a wolfling, there was no
one watching who could not know, no plans that could be
upset or reputations that could suffer."

"Except your own, unless you planned never to return," Odhinn said. "Was that your plan?"

"Perhaps," Brynhild admitted. "I did not want to return. I thought that I would remain with the Volsungs for
some time, that I would have a child of my own and
simply, quietly follow Sigmund and Signy into the elf-
world. Yes, that was what I did want."

"You thought to allow circumstances to decide what you were afraid to decide for yourself," Odhinn said, watching her closely. "Would it be of any comfort to you for me to say that I have known and understood? That I was even prepared to grant your desire? I do not like it. I love you enough to feel possessive of you, but I also care for you enough to allow you any happiness that you might find. But I could never allow you to bring any wolfling children into the world. That world, at least. And I should have warned you."

Brynhild looked at him in surprise. "But why? My children will have my powers. . . ."

"My dear girl, that is the very reason!" Odhinn exclaimed. "I created the Volsungs for the single purpose of winning the ring from Fafnir. If I wanted wolflings with the powers of Valkyries, I would have spared myself the trouble and simply sent you to fetch it for me. Do you not recall why I could not allow that?"

He made a helpless gesture. "It hardly matters now. Siggier knows where the Volsungs are, and he is on his way to destroy them. To complicate the matter, Jordh has intervened yet again. She has forbidden any of us to help the Volsungs. We may have them back—or at least their spirits—once the matter has resolved itself. Also, she has declared that the child you carry must be destroyed."

"My child?" she asked fearfully.

Odhinn nodded. "It must be done, for the sake of the Volsungs. I would permit you to keep your child if I could, but Jordh demands it. And I cannot protect you from her. As for your own fate, you will remain here until the matter is resolved, and then you will go to join your friends in the elf-world."

"You will grant me leave to go?" she asked.

"Grant you?" he demanded, staring at her. "I am not offering you any choice. You are dismissed from your regular duties as a Valkyrie; you still possess your powers, but not the authority to use them. You have defied me twice, so how can I trust you now? You may call it leave to go, if that is what you want. But there is no element of choice involved; you are both dismissed and banished.''

Brynhild looked so stunned and dismayed that he laughed at her. ''My dear, silly girl, do not look so stricken! You seem, in the course of your duties guarding the wolflings, to have acquired a wolfling's heart. Brynhild, with your powers, you will be the queen of the Wolves of Alfheim. Which is a good thing, for you are now a most worthless Valkyrie. For your own peace of mind, look upon this as a reward rather than a condemnation.''

Brynhild turned to leave, then paused. She looked back hesitantly. ''My lord, what of your own plans?''

''There are now hundreds of Volsungs in Alfheim, so there is no problem in that regard,'' Odhinn replied thoughtfully. ''Many, of course, have been re-animated and may never return. That is why Sigmund and Signy must leave Midgardh alive, so that they might some day return, and so that they can retain possession of the sword. Together they have the potential for being the best warriors their race has ever produced, and you must teach them to work as one to command the sword to its highest potential.''

''Then I may continue to serve you?''

He shrugged. ''If that is what you wish.''

Brynhild glanced down shyly. ''I have made mistakes, but never in open defiance of you. I always believed that what I was doing was for the best.''

Odhinn nodded. ''So I thought, or I would not have been forgiving. But do not fear, for you will serve me better among the Wolves of Alfheim. I have Valkyries to spare, but you will be unique. And I hope that once you find the satisfaction you seek, then you will recall that the greatest of the powers in your possession has always been your wisdom.''

Waiting was the hardest part of any battle, especially so for one who had always stormed forth to meet challenges head-on, even violently. Waiting was hardest for her, knowing the danger that was about to befall her friends and unable to do a thing to stop it. She went to Idhunn, and her pregnancy was ended quickly and simply, although she was left in her new form. After that she went to her apartment in the Valkyries' barracks . . . having no other place to go. She thought that she might cry over the loss of her child; she had been doing that a lot lately, often for no reason that she could understand. But this time, curiously, she did not. She began packing for her journey to Alfheim, only to realize that none of her things would fit. Annoyed, she did assemble a full suit of Valkyrie's armor from spare parts in the armory, and she made a point of wearing it at all times. She realized that she must look like a little wolfling pretending to be a Valkyrie, but she felt more secure.

Asgardh seemed like a prison to her now, and she could not wait to be away from its confining walls. This place had never really been home to her, just a place to come between her rounds. And so it was that five long days passed while she paced and brooded her fate like a caged wolf. Those who had known her before hardly recognized her for the person she had been, and everyone stayed well away from her. And then the time came at last that Sigrune, Captain of the Valkyries, came to her.

''Soon it will be done,'' she said. ''Siggier has discovered the northern hall of the Volsungs and will be closing in before nightfall.''

''And the wolflings?'' Brynhild asked apprehensively. ''Do they know of their danger?''

"No, they do not," the Valkyrie said. "I fear that they will be caught, for Siggier is very good at weaving his traps."

Brynhild was so distracted that she barely mumbled her thanks, then retired again to her apartment to consider this matter. She almost wished that the two wolflings would perish, for they would be restored to life but could never again be involved in Odhinn's plans. But she was fearful of what might happen to Odhinn's plans if they should be captured alive, and Siggier would have the magic sword again in his possession whether he took them alive or dead. Either way, Brynhild did not want them to suffer.

There seemed only one answer, one that might work if she moved quickly and quietly. And if it failed . . . she was already banished from her former duties, soon to be exiled. She was risking her own life if Jordh caught her, but at least Odhinn could not be made to share in her punishment. And she was acting to protect his plans as much as she wished to spare the Volsungs. She made her decision and hurried down to the stables, where she immediately began saddling Glaerfaxi.

"Soon you will be leaving this place forever," the horse remarked, finding her thoughts easy to follow.

"I will not return here ever again," Brynhild said.

The great horse lowered her head, her ears twitching. "I have thought about it much, since I heard that you must leave. I have decided that I must go with you. I doubt that I will be of much service, but some, perhaps. I do not doubt that I will enjoy it, either way."

"You might have cause to reconsider that," Brynhild warned. "I am going to save the Volsungs, whatever I must do."

"And there is, of course, a reason why this must be done?"

"Sigmund and Signy are special," Brynhild insisted.

"The best ever. And their unborn son will be better still. Odhinn desperately wants them saved, but he is himself helpless to do anything, and he cannot ask me to take the risk that he cannot assume himself. But I am willing. I need your help."

"We are spirits of power," Glaerfaxi pointed out thoughtfully. "If we are destroyed, we cannot be easily re-animated. There may be nothing left when Jordh is done."

"That is why it must be your free choice."

"Then I will do it, and may fate look kindly upon me," Glaerfaxi said, deciding quickly. "It's a good thing that I am willing to follow you into exile."

"The Allfather would not hold you to blame," Brynhild protested.

"I am not a horse to be ridden with bit and stirrup," Glaerfaxi replied. "I am a person. I am able to decide for myself, and I could refuse."

Minutes later the pair began their final descent into the valley that held the northern holding of the Volsungs. They had already located Siggier and his men an hour or less to the southwest, marching unerringly toward their goal. This was the beginning of the dangerous part of their plan, the point at which their disobedience would become apparent. Brynhild had first hoped to get the wolflings out of Midhgardh and to safety in Alfheim, but that was impossible. At least she could deliver her warning and be gone again in moments. She did have faith that, duly warned, the two Volsungs could take care of themselves.

The horse pulled herself out of her quick descent and landed lightly, trotting to a stop before the main door. There was no problem about finding the wolflings, for they were outside even before the Valkyrie could dismount. At least they did know her, for she was still the same Brynhild beneath her new silver armor.

"Brynhild, you have returned!" Signy exclaimed.

"It will not be for very long," Brynhild said. "Listen well. I have been banished from Asgardh. I will be a wolfling forever now, and join you in the elf-world."

"You do not sound displeased about it," Sigmund remarked. "But am I to understand that we will be going into the elf-world immediately?"

"No, it will not be that simple," she said. "I fear that I do not have time to explain everything. Know this. Siggier is on his way. He and his warriors are almost here, and they mean to trap you. The Allfather and I would protect you if we could. But there is a third will at work in this, one that we cannot oppose. This, I regret, is the deal. If you survive, then you must go immediately into the elf-world. If you die, then the Allfather will re-animate your spirits and send you there all the same. It might seem all the same to you, but Siggier will make you suffer if he can, and he must not regain the sword in any case."

"I take it that you were not supposed to have brought this warning?" Signy asked suspiciously.

"No, my own existence is at risk," she admitted. "But I still had to come."

"And now that you have warned us?"

"I must get out of this place as quickly as I can, before my presence is noticed. Flee while you can, south and west of this place. I will never be far away, and I will help you if I can, should things go badly. But, for your own sake, you must save yourselves if you can. Trust in the sword."

With that she leaped back into her saddle and was away.

"Odhinn, the time is almost at hand."

The words echoed through the empty halls of Valhalla, causing the guardian wolves to leap up in alarm. Odhinn glanced up in annoyance.

"I know very well what time it is," he said, hoping that

Jordh would either state her intentions or go away. "Is not my personal shame and my dismay for the lives of my children enough for you?"

"Were my warnings not enough for you?" Jordh asked in return. "What is the purpose in defying me for the sake of defiance? Shed me no tears for the children of the wolves, when you would send Brynhild to certain doom."

"Brynhild is there for a purpose," Odhinn said impatiently. "When the battle is done, she will take the wolflings from your realm. You did, at least, grant me that."

"I am well aware of Brynhild's purpose," Jordh said. "She went straight to the Volsungs and warned them. Then she retreated into the hills as if nothing had happened. You always presume that I am inattentive."

"She warned the Volsungs?" Odhinn asked.

"You do not seem greatly surprised to hear it."

"No, it does not surprise me," Odhinn said thoughtfully. "I realize it now, that it is exactly what I should have expected her to do. She has already disobeyed me twice for the sake of the Volsungs, and she has been banished for it."

"Banished?"

"Yes, banished!" Odhinn snapped. "I have dismissed her from her duties. She is to accompany the Volsungs to Alfheim to live as a wolfling forever."

"Then listen to me well!" Jordh declared. "Brynhild will disobey again. Things will not go so smoothly as she may wish, and she will surely take some direct action to protect the Volsungs. Already they have two advantages: the sword and Brynhild's warning. If she interferes again, then you must be there to even the odds. You will take away that which you gave long ago. You will destroy the sword, so that Sigmund must face his enemy with nothing that is not his own."

"But that will surely mean his death!" Odhinn protested.

"So it must be," Jordh agreed coldly. "Also, Signy must go back to Siggier, for by the laws of his people she is his. Whether he would kill her or keep her, her life is his."

Odhinn turned away and said nothing.

"I am willing to forget the warning that Brynhild has already given," Jordh continued. "If she interferes again, then she shall be punished. If she tries to save the Volsungs and fails, then you shall punish her for her disobedience. If she succeeds, then she will forfeit her life to me. To save Brynhild, you must now protect her from herself."

CHAPTER FOURTEEN

Night was beginning to fall as Siggier's party began the last ascent into the mountains. Ahead lay the broad valley they had seen from the previous ridge, carved deep into the fabric of the mountains. Tall stands of trees and grassy meadows filled the valley, a green, peaceful refuge in the barren heights. One more ridge and he would order his warriors to sweep out and draw a ring around the quiet holding that rested deep within the valley.

He had never expected to hear of the two children of Sigi again, for he had thought they fled this world with the rest of their kind. He had hoped, silently to himself, that they were gone forever. For him it was a closed matter. They had left him alive when they could have slain him, helpless under his own spell. He even admired their determination and resourcefulness. Another, deeper part of him wanted Signy back. Once she was gone, he had found, to his surprise, that he had loved her in his own rough way and he still did. But this was the task before him, and it demanded his attention. He would kill the Volsungs when he found them, quickly and simply, with no games to satisfy a vengeance that had no meaning. Then, perhaps, he would have peace.

Siggier paused and waited when he spied Trigin racing

back downhill. The big weasel weaved among the rocks, his back bent in an exaggerated bow to bring his legs closer together for better speed. The landvaeta leaped to the top of a rock before his lord and began bobbing his head in some feral salute.

"Lord Siggier, it is done," Trigin announced. "They are waiting for you at the top of the ridge."

"They know we are coming?" Siggier asked sharply, plainly implying that the scout had failed in his duties.

"Yes, Lord, they knew. They were waiting long before we reached this place. They have been warned. Perhaps they heard. Perhaps they saw."

"That will make trapping them even more difficult," Siggier said absently, then looked down at the weasel. "Have six archers separate from the group and move uphill under cover. Remind them to stay downwind."

"Ambush?"

"Yes. Shoot to kill," he instructed, then turned to face uphill. He needed to end this quickly; darkness was falling, and that would work only to the wolflings' advantage. He knew that he could not surround and corner them, so his only hope was to somehow draw them out for his archers. If they ran, he would lose them. A pack of wolfhounds might run them down, but all he had was a weasel.

"Volsungs!" he called out. "Volsungs, I want to talk to you."

"I want to talk to you," Sigmund responded, although he did not show himself. "Come on up the hill alone."

Siggier hesitated only an instant. Only a fool would accept such an invitation, unless it came from a Volsung. As he neared the top, he saw that Sigmund had chosen this place well. If his soldiers tried to rush this barren, crumbling pile of slabs and boulders, they would need some time to reach the top and would arrive winded, only to find the wolflings a mile away by then. Similarly, in the growing darkness, his archers would have to steal almost to the top to find their marks.

He found the Volsungs waiting on a flat, open space at the top of the rise. Sigmund waited near the center, his sword drawn, while Signy sat to one side with a drawn bow. She looked at him as he reached the top, a cold but otherwise unreadable expression that frightened him. He did not doubt that had she been mortal, she would have used her bow at that moment.

He turned quickly to Sigmund. "I have come. What do you want to say to me, son of Sigi?"

"A proposition," Sigmund replied. "Let this contest remain between you and me, and we will settle it with our swords . . . alone."

Siggier stroked his mustache thoughtfully as he watched the Volsung closely. "Why should I agree to that?"

"For two reasons," the Volsung answered. "First, this is a purely personal matter between you and me. We have long fought for possession of the Sword of Asgardh and for Signy. You have always been above the ways of ordinary men and I am hardly human. But let us settle this matter, as they say, like men."

"I understand what you would imply, although you obviously do not understand it yourself. What is the second reason?"

Sigmund shrugged. "If you do not agree, then this will become a personal matter between you and Signy, and she will put an arrow through you where you stand."

Siggier glanced at the wolfling in mock surprise. "Surely you would not do such a thing to me!"

"Gladly," Signy replied, drawing her bow tighter. "You see, I slew my own children for less reason."

"Ah, so it was you!" Siggier exclaimed. "But why?"

"It was a test to see if there was even a measure of wolfling in them. They failed."

Siggier paused, deciding that he was in a very precarious position. He did not underestimate either the abilities of the wolflings or the powers of that sword. He was not certain that he could defeat Sigmund, and he doubted that Signy would simply let him go if he did. To survive, he had to delay long enough for his archers to move into position.

"What if I simply let you go?" he suggested.

Sigmund shook his head. "I cannot let you go. For us to be free, then I must fight you."

"I really did not expect that it could end otherwise," Siggier said as he drew his sword and advanced.

Their blades met with a flash, and Siggier was surprised to see his own come away deeply notched. His blade was of the finest steel known to mortal smiths, but it was no match against the strength of the magic sword. Still, he saw that Sigmund was slow to react. The wolfling was shorter, lighter by nearly half, with less reach. Siggier thought that if he pressed an attack quickly enough, he might even be able to defeat the Volsung. But even as he conceived that plan, he also became aware that the advantage was turning against him. Sigmund remained mostly on the defensive, but no mortal attack could get past his sword, which moved of its own will to block any thrust or blow.

Lightning suddenly rent the sky almost directly above them. The three looked up in surprise that a roiling thunderstorm was moving down the valley of the Volsung holding, its mists already encircling the rocky hill on which they stood. Then Sigmund and Siggier returned to their contest with renewed determination, and Signy was too distracted by the battle to see the archers crouching not fifty paces from where she stood. They drew their bows, waiting for the next flash of lightning to sight their prey.

The next instant bolts of lightning racked across the slopes of the ridge, striking with deadly accuracy the archers who waited in hiding as well as the warriors gathered at the bottom. Brynhild lifted her spear, its point still glowing, as Glaerfaxi circled down.

"Strike, Sigmund! Trust in the sword!" she called above the rising wind, encouraging the Volsung to press his advantage.

But Glaerfaxi sheared away, retreating in haste. The approaching storm split apart, illuminated from within by rippling flashes of lightning, as Sleipnir hurtled down out of the rift. Odhinn lowered his spear and a bolt of light shot from its tip to strike full upon Sigmund's sword. The blade glowed and shimmered and snapped apart with explosive force.

Both Sigmund and Siggier fell back startled from the blast. Siggier recovered first, although half blinded by the flash, drawing back his sword with both hands. The weaponless Volsung shifted quickly to his animal form and tried to spring away, but his opponent's blade came down across his back, biting deep enough to sever his spine. Signy's arrow caught Siggier in the chest, jerking him away only an instant too late. The two warriors fell dead to the ground almost as one.

Sleipnir cut to one side, the speed of his flight too great for him to land, and circled back through the storm to slow for another pass. Glaerfaxi was quicker, spiralling down to the hilltop and stopping directly before the stunned Signy. The wolfling girl looked up as the horse's bulk cut off her sight of her brother's body. Brynhild held out an impatient hand to pull her into the saddle.

"Come!" Brynhild ordered. "I take you to join him in Alfheim."

Signy extended her hand uncertainly. Brynhild took her by the wrist and lifted her easily onto the horse's back. Glaerfaxi leaped into the air before they were even settled, and she was barely in the sky before Sleipnir began to drop again toward the hilltop. Paying no heed to the departing figures, he landed lightly on a low rise overlooking the bodies of the two warriors. Odhinn slipped down from his saddle and stood looking down at the ruins of his hopes and careful plans, leaning heavily on his spear.

"Behold how even the best intentions and thorough plans may go awry, turning in upon themselves until they become a mirror image of what they were meant to be," Jordh said from one side. "For all the great powers that you and I have in our possession, I am awed at how much power rests in mere circumstance."

"Circumstance?" Odhinn asked harshly. "This was all of your planning."

"No, indeed it was not," Jordh insisted. "The echoes of our deeds never die. This is not yet over, my friend. What of Brynhild?"

She paused, and even Odhinn looked up as the Valkyrie's horn call echoed through the mountains. Every ear within this realm, and every immortal ear within the nine realms, would hear that resounding summons. Brynhild was calling the Valkyries to her aid.

"Brynhild is loyal," Jordh remarked. "She means to save Signy for you in spite of your orders. Such disobedience cannot go unpunished."

"Have you not had vengeance enough?" Odhinn demanded bitterly.

"Vengeance is of no interest to me," she said. "Now the choice is yours. Destroy Signy, so that the children of Sigi need never bother me again. Or punish Brynhild for her disobedience. Strip her of her powers and leave her exposed to the mortal world, for any man to claim who would have her. Let the proud Valkyrie be reduced to a mortal wife.''

In the mountains where the world-gate stood, not far from the world-tree, was a towering, barren peak of rock where the Valkyries gathered at need. Every world had such a place where they would know to meet and gather in an emergency. The echoes of Brynhild's horn call were only beginning to fade as the Valkyries began to converge on that place, turning from their many paths.

The first to arrive was Ranngird, the smallest of the Valkyries, whose duty it was to watch the gate of Asgardh. She sprang to her waiting horse and dropped through the main world-gate over the bridge Bifrost. After that, the journey to the peak was only a short leap for her powerful steed. She landed on a short ledge beneath the summit and sent her horse out of the way, then ran up to the very peak to greet the others as they came in.

Almost immediately the Valkyries began to converge on the towering peak. They ran openly, ready for battle, enveloping themselves in rolling mists that formed into threatening thunderstorms, illuminated from within by rippling sheets of lightning. The first came from the northwest, streaking over the darkened land. A second, larger mass descended from true north, their paths converging to approach the peak from above. Ranngird could see the distant flashes of a third, moving in quickly from over the sea. The first was upon her in moments. Ranngird released her helmet and pulled it off, then raised her spear in salute.

"Hail, Helmgird! Descend to the peak!"

The rolling mass of clouds paused almost directly overhead, and a moment later the tiny figures of horse and rider dropped out of the dark mass, circling around to land. The horse pulled to a quick stop on the landing below the peak as Helmgird pulled off her helmet.

"Hail, Ranngird! What trouble awaits?" she called to the waiting Valkyrie.

"I do not know. Brynhild sent the call but has not arrived." The little Valkyrie turned back to the clouds. "Hail, Valthora! Noble Sverdhleif!"

A pair of mounts and riders broke from underneath the storm. The horses circled closely, straining to break the speed of their flight. They landed at a run, pausing just long enough for their riders to leap off before moving downhill to get out of the way. Already Skogull was descending toward the peak, coming straight down from her westerly approach.

"Hail, Ranngird! What news do you have?" Sverdhleif called up.

"Patience, Sverdhleif. I do not know. Sigrune approaches. Perhaps she will know."

Two more masses of boiling clouds were hurtling toward them through the night sky. Lightning flashed from within the gray bulks of the storms, briefly illuminating the land below. Sigrune raced through the converging clouds, while Geirahod and Ranverd rode together from out of the northwest. The racing clouds met overhead, joining with the mass of storms already gathered. Three riders dropped out of the clouds at almost the same instant, circling down.

Ranngird lifted her spear to salute her captain, more delighted with these happenings than apprehensive. The others below her lifted their own spears, and the three riders returned that salute as they made the final descent. Ranngird abandoned her post, hurrying down to join the others.

Sigrune leaped down, handing Helmgird her spear so that she could pull off her helmet. She glanced quickly about the group, and it was certain from her expression that she was in no way amused. The others had come looking for battle, certain that they could handle anything as a group. Now they understood that this was no game.

"Where is Brynhild? Was that not her call?" she asked impatiently.

"Indeed it was," Ranngird offered. "I heard it clearly."

"Is she in danger?" Valthora asked.

"That I do not doubt, although I do not yet know who she may fear," Sigrune said, then quickly explained what she could of the situation. The Valkyries were dismayed.

"We cannot fight Jordh!" Sverdhleif protested.

"If not Jordh, then the Allfather himself," Sigrune explained. "Or so I read it. Jordh would have destroyed her outright. I will not compel, nor even ask, any of you to remain. But I must do what I can to help her."

"She comes!" Skogull announced, having taken Ranngird's place on the summit.

Brynhild was nearly there before they were even aware of her. Unlike the others, Glaerfaxi flew in oddly low and slow, without the violent battleclouds. Everything suggested that she was trying to avoid being seen, although they did not understand why the horse did not fly faster if Brynhild had been hurt. Glaerfaxi climbed to match the height of the peak, and as she circled around to land, they saw that she carried a passenger who would not have been fully protected by the steed's magic at higher speed.

Not a mortal, Sigrune realized, but a wolfling. Signy, in fact, she saw as Glaerfaxi landed on the ledge and trotted to a stop. Sigrune waited as the others helped the silent Volsung down, then took Brynhild by one arm and drew her off to one side.

"Brynhild, what have you done?" she demanded, then paused. Glaerfaxi was peering over her shoulder, but the horse was a part of this. "Have you defied Jordh to the point of open battle?"

"No, not Jordh. Odhinn himself," Brynhild answered, then quickly explained what she had done.

"Bryn, listen to me carefully now," Sigrune said sternly when she was done. "You are going to need all of your considerable wits to salvage anything out of this, so you had better remember where you put them. What will you do now?"

"Me?" Brynhild asked. "Why, I have to stay here. Signy must be taken alive into the elf-world. If Odhinn finds her here, then he will surely destroy her. The most important thing now is that she must survive."

"Why?" Sigrune demanded, mystified.

"So that her child will live," Brynhild answered. "Do not ask, but believe me when I say that the prophecy of the Nornir holds that he will help to save the nine realms from destruction. Signy must be delivered safely to the elves. I will stay here and endure Odhinn's wrath. That is the only way that I can delay him."

"Come along, then," Sigrune said and turned back to the group. "Ranngird, you go to Vikfjallaland and find the spirit of the Volsung Sigmund. Get him to Asgardh immediately, and mind you get the right one . . . and stay well away from Odhinn!"

"Why me?" Ranngird protested weakly.

"Because I told you to. Move! I want him found five minutes ago." She paused to survey the rest of the group. "Ranverd, you and Valthora take Signy to Alfheim. Deliver her directly into the care of King Alflysa himself. Tell him that the Allfather wills it, and that it's more important than he can imagine."

"Will you not take her?" Brynhild asked.

"No, Ranverd is better," Sigrune replied. "She has the Alfheim run and can likely handle the elves better than I. Besides, you will need me here." She looked up at the guard on the summit. "Warn me when you see Odhinn."

"He is coming," Skogull called back.

Paying no heed, Brynhild quickly extracted Signy from the watchful Valkyries and drew her off to one side. The wolfling moved woodenly at first, still shocked by what had happened. Then she became aware of who she was with.

"Brynhild, what are you doing?" she protested. "I want to go to Sigmund."

"I am sending you to him now," Brynhild said. "My sisters will take you to the elf-world, and Sigmund will be there soon. Someday you will join him in the forests of that world, but for now you must remain with the elves. Remember that you are the last Volsung of Midhgardh."

"I have had enough of being the Allfather's tool!" she declared. "What can I do? The sword is broken."

"The sword can be renewed," Brynhild said. "One day another Volsung will take up the task, and the Wanderer will give him the sword. Sigmund is gone from this realm and can never return. It remains for his son to do what he was not allowed."

"Son?" Signy asked, looking up. "Will I have a son?"

"Yes, I promise it," Brynhild insisted. "When the winter is past and the first days of spring return to the forests of the elf-world, then your son will be born. He will be tall, with dark eyes and brown hair streaked with black."

"Our son," Signy said softly, then looked up in fear. "Save me, friend. Save my son."

Brynhild nodded. "Odhinn is coming, and we are both marked for his vengeance. I have arranged for you to flee to safety. I will stay here and divert Odhinn's wrath to myself alone."

"You cannot flee with me now?" Signy asked. "Is it that important to you?"

"It is," Brynhild assured her. "I once carried a child, half-sister to your own. She could not survive, so it is even

more important to me that your own must. I do not know
what is to become of me, but I believe that I will be here
to greet your son when he returns. Give him this name,
Sigurdh, that I will know him when he comes.''

"So it shall be," Signy promised, smiling and weeping
at once. "Someday you will find him again, and he will
tell you of my gratitude.''

"Hurry now," the Valkyrie said, taking her by the hand
and leading her to where Ranverd waited in her saddle.
Brynhild and Sigrune lifted her up to the back of the tall
horse. Signy settled herself as best she could, placing both
hands about Ranverd's armored waist. The horse ran to the
edge of the shelf and leaped off, followed a moment later
by Valthora. They headed due east, at a right angle to
Odhinn's path, keeping as low as the rugged terrain would
permit.

A moment later the vast, threatening shape of a raging
storm began to rise over the bulk of the summit as Odhinn
descended upon the waiting Valkyries. Skogull hurried
down to join the others. The hurtling mass of clouds
continued to approach, larger and more threatening than
any the Valkyries might summon to hide their approach.

Brynhild hastened to her steed. "Foxy, get yourself out
of here.''

Glaerfaxi only shook her head. "My guilt is equal to
your own, for it was my choice as well. I will share your
punishment. You will need me.''

The racing mass of clouds collided with the dark, hovering bulk overhead, the drifting remnants of the Valkyries'
passage. The entire rolling bank of clouds exploded in
fury, bolts of angry lightning ripping through its entire
length. Sleipnir's odd shape dropped from beneath the
clouds, descended almost straight down toward the peak.
Then he turned and continued in a tight spiral, circling
wide on his final pass before landing on the ledge.

The Valkyries drew back defensively, shielding Brynhild behind them, as Odhinn leaped down from his horse. He stood before them, as dark and menacing as the storm overhead, silent as he looked from first one to the other as if to search their hearts and minds for disloyalty.

"Spare me your petty tricks," he declared. "Let Brynhild stand forth."

The Valkyries parted to let one of their number through, but it was Sigrune who stepped out from the group to stand before him. "My lord, I am the Captain of your warrior-maidens, and therefore responsible for them. I must know what Brynhild has done to offend you, so that the full truth may be known in this matter."

"Do you mock me?" Odhinn demanded in anger. "I never appointed you the keeper of my conscience, nor did I ever surrender to you my right to order or reprimand my own servants."

"That is the truth," Sigrune agreed. "And yet, by all we know, Brynhild sought only to serve you, taking upon herself risks that you could not ask of her. Why do you seek to punish such devotion?"

"Hear then the truth in this matter," Odhinn said. "Stand forth, Brynhild. Are you too frightened to face the responsibility for what you have done?"

Brynhild stepped calmly through the group to stand at her captain's side. "I am not afraid, for I knew the punishment I risked. Tell me the punishment that you have decreed, but tell me also of what I am guilty."

Startled by her insolence, Odhinn stared at her. "If you expect to be punished for your deeds, then you are aware of your crimes. You are three times guilty of disobedience. Three times you thought that you knew better than I how to manage my affairs.

"Listen, you Valkyries, to your sister's crimes!" he declared sharply. "Brynhild has contrived to cause the

Volsung Signy to destroy her own mortal children. For this she was forgiven. I sent her to guard the Volsungs, but she disregarded her duty and allowed herself to be made pregnant by the wolfling Sigmund. For this she was banished from the Valkyries, to remain a wolfling forever in the forest of Alfheim. Lastly I ordered her not to interfere in the affairs of the Volsungs, neither to warn them of the dangers they faced nor to defend them, and yet she did both.

"This time there will be nothing benign to the punishment I decree. I trust that you will learn something from this and never again fail me with disobedience. Now go! Return to your nightly rounds and serve me well, for any who fail again will share Brynhild's fate."

The storm overhead was split with searing bolts of lightning in response to his anger. The Valkyries hesitated only a moment, then turned and raced downhill to claim their horses. Odhinn turned away, leaning heavily upon his spear. Brynhild, alone and downcast, laid down her helmet and spear on the barren rock then waited in silence for her fate. A moment later the storm rumbled again and she turned to see the Valkyries take to the air, fleeing in haste.

Odhinn remained silent for some time, leaving Brynhild to wonder at his thoughts, if he was fighting anger or regret or indecision. She knew that her punishment was a certainty, and in spite of her resolve, she was terribly afraid. As she waited the wind returned almost shyly from the north, gently dispersing the storm and carrying it slowly away. The night deepened.

"What have you done, Brynhild?" Odhinn asked at last. "What did you hope to accomplish? Did you not realize that the Volsungs had a better chance without your interference? You could have been with them in Alfheim. You could have lived in peace."

"I know," Brynhild agreed. "I saw one last chance to salvage something for you, and I did what I had to do."

"What have you done for me? Sigmund cannot return, and Signy is of little use without him. The sword is gone as well. Nothing remains."

"Their child remains," Brynhild said softly. "The sword can be renewed. One last chance."

A distant flash of lightning illuminated the night sky far to the north. Brynhild saw it and was encouraged, for her risk had been worthwhile. Odhinn saw it as well. He stared north for a long moment before turning to her.

"Sigrune signals you. What is it she would tell you?" he demanded, although gently. "Your plan has worked, has it now? Signy is safe in Alfheim, where she was meant to be. And you gave her that chance by staying behind to distract me."

Brynhild looked down and did not answer.

"It was a noble effort, but you have again outsmarted yourself," he said distantly. "Jordh has anticipated this. She has demanded that Signy and her son be destroyed, or you must be stripped of your powers and left a simple wolfling, for any man who finds you to claim as his wife."

Brynhild lowered her eyes and nodded slowly. "I accept the punishment."

For a breathless instant those words seemed to hang heavily in the air. Odhinn turned slowly, looked upon her with surprise and even awe. Aware that he was watching her, Brynhild glanced up at him, then slowly straightened to stand tall and proud before him. She saw now the one chance remaining for herself, and she would fight for it. As clearly as if the Nornir had shown her the days to come, she knew what she had to do, what she had dimly known when she had sent Signy away.

"The choice is made," she said. "Signy will live, and

so will her son. I will accept the punishment. I misunderstood your councils, misled by my own heart. I have failed you, and in payment I give you the son of Sigmund and Signy, even if I must pay for his life with my own. Name my punishment."

Odhinn watched her intently. "If this is your choice, then so it must be. You shall be stripped of your Valkyrie powers, and I will lay upon you a protective sleep until the first man to find you claims you for his own. You will ride no more, nor enjoy the pride and privileges of the great ones."

Brynhild considered that for a moment. "So it shall be, but one thing I would ask. If I must give up all that I have been, then I ask that the man who finds me be brave and fearless, an exceptional man. Leave me here on the peak, and surround it in flames only a hero would dare pass."

Odhinn turned away. "You ask to much! Your punishment has been declared by another, and I dare not challenge that."

"Why should the full punishment be given, if I have still failed?" Brynhild insisted. "Sigmund is gone, and the sword is gone. I will not be with the Volsungs I love or have the freedom I desire. Nor shall I ever again ride with my sisters, nor stand by your high seat in Valhalla and serve your drink on the nights of celebration. If my own pride and joy must be stripped from me, then at least allow me to be given to a man in whom I can find some small pride and joy. I would rather face death itself."

"The fate you were given was meant to be worse than death to you," Odhinn said without turning to look at her. "But I will grant your desire. If Jordh is displeased, then she can remove the flames and leave you naked and alone to the fate she intended. That is all I can grant."

"That is all I can ask."

Odhinn turned to Sleipnir, who looked up and lifted his

ears attentively. "Bespeak the guardian of the Gate of Asgardh, and have Loki sent to me. Then await me below this ledge."

Sleipnir nodded and hurried off. Odhinn remained as he stood, bent wearily as he leaned upon his spear, his back to the Valkyrie. She watched him eagerly for some sign of displeasure or regret, wondering if he would ever be grateful to her for saving his plans, or if he would miss her in the years to come. She only wanted that they should not make this final parting under the darkness of his wrath.

"I have failed you, my lord," she said softly. "I am sorry, I never meant for things to turn out this way."

He did not reply, staring off into the south. The storm was passing swiftly out of sight among the distant mountains, quick flashes of lightning causing its dark mass to glow from within. Sleipnir returned and waited quietly on the slope below. Loki was near, but discreetly out of sight. The time had come. Odhinn laid his spear against the side of a large boulder and stood for a moment staring down at its gleaming head.

"Reconsider, Brynhild," he said at last. "I am not defeated. Let this wolfling meet her fate. I will see that she joins her twin, and they will be happy. Accept the life that I offered you before."

Brynhild looked up, at first startled. "My lord, this is far greater than I deserve. But I must refuse. I have promised my service to you, and I have promised Signy her life. And yet, even though my future is dark, I believe that I may serve you yet where I have failed you before. Some day a warrior will come for me and awaken me from my long sleep, and then who can foresee the wondrous things we might do!"

Odhinn understood at last the full vision of the future that she saw and knew just who was the one she willingly awaited, and he was moved by her devotion. "Farewell, my child. Now we must part, and I fear that it is not in our fates to ever meet again. I hope that you may find the happiness and freedom you seek. I could never give you those things, as much as I tried. A new future awaits you, so make of it what you wish. And it may be that you will one day find the happiness you seek with one who is freer than I."

He stood for a moment, staring absently at the stars. Brynhild sensed his hesitation and spared him the distress of having to force her punishment upon her. She approached him slowly, silently, until she stood only a couple of paces behind him. He turned quickly, as if suddenly aware of her closeness, and took her firmly in his arms. For a long moment he held her close as he worked the subtle magic that subdued her powers. Then he gently forced her to look up and stared down into her eyes, deep, clear eyes that were devoid of fear but full of life and hope.

Then her eyes closed, and she fell lifelessly into his arms. He held her inert form against him, as if that final act had robbed him of both strength and resolve, before lifting her up to cradle her tiny wolfling form in his arms. She slept quietly, even peacefully, her face so tranquil and composed that he could hardly bear to look down at her.

"Farewell," he said a final time.

Then he turned and began the slow climb to the summit of the rocky peak, while Glaerfaxi followed silently and unnoticed. Odhinn never looked up from the limp burden in his arms. He laid her on the cold stone just below the summit. A small fir, moved by his magic, broke its seed and, within moments, pushed branches out from a crack in the rock, spreading wide to offer her some protection.

"When the sunlight again touches the lid of your soft eyes, then they shall open," he said, completing the spell of her enchantment. "But it shall be another they behold, not I."

He rose slowly and took Brynhild's helmet from where she had laid it aside with her spear, and returned with both to where she lay. Gently and carefully he slipped her hair down inside the collar of her armor, then set the helmet over her head and locked it down. He rose to leave and saw Glaerfaxi standing behind him as if for the first time. He had never thought to include the horse in his punishment, but he saw clearly that she wanted to remain. Odhinn led her to a level place on the slope near her mistress and laid one hand gently on her head between her eyes. She braced her legs and lowered her head almost to the ground and passed into an enchanted sleep. She seemed almost to turn to stone, become a statue of herself, not even the hairs of her mane or tail moving in the night breeze.

Odhinn left them reluctantly, moving slowly down the steep, rocky slope to where Sleipnir waited in silence. He turned and stood for a moment gazing longingly back up to where the Valkyrie lay. Sleipnir stood beside him, sharing his grief. With sudden, painful resolve he lifted his spear over his head. The point glowed fiercely, radiating a golden, burning light. The air was still, waiting, as he invoked Loki's power, shaped by his own and channeled through the spear.

"Loki, hear!
Answer me clear!
Of the flames you were made
in long ages past;
Now guard well this mountain
and surround it in flames
that never die.

> Arise, and lend me your strength!
> Encircle this summit in flame!
> Loki! Loki! Arise!''

Thus Odhinn invoked the magic fire. A golden glow
became visible behind the peak and flickering tongues of
flame appeared from either side, crawling along a natural
path in the stone just below the first ledge. At length they
met in the middle, and a sheet of flame leaped up to form
an impenetrable barrier. Odhinn held aloft his spear a final
time, and the point again glowed with a fierce radiance.

> ''Who fears not the power of my spear
> Alone shall pass the flames!''

And so the invocation was complete, and the glow faded
from his spear. He lowered it slowly, absently as he
continued to stare up at the peak. He was alone now,
feeling as if he had thrown away the last thing in his life
that had true meaning. Sleipnir nudged him gently. Odhinn
laid a hand on the horse's head, then sat down wearily to
watch the flames through the night. Brynhild had sold her
very life for a final chance to serve him, and she had not
regretted it. Now he wondered if he had given away
something even more important. Now that it was done, he
felt only defeat.

The ring of fire burned steadily like a golden crown
upon the old mountain's lofty head, a radiant beacon
against the night sky.

Signy stood alone in her comfortable room in the palace
of King Alflysa of the elves. Morning had come, and her
thoughts were a little better collected, and she began to
think seriously about all that had happened. Brynhild had
not come for her, and she feared the worst for the brave

Valkyrie. Sigmund was likely somewhere in the forests of the elf-world by that time, telling the pack of their adventures. She wished that she could go to him, but she also understood why she could not. After a time she left her room and went outside to sit in the garden just beyond.

She had not been sitting long when she became aware that she was not alone. She turned to see the Wanderer standing a few paces away, quietly waiting for her. He had come so quickly and silently that she wondered at first if this was only an illusion. Then she caught his scent, underlaid with both wolfling and horse. She smelled Sigmund on him, and that surprised her. But Sigmund was not there. She drew back.

"Do not fear me," he said gently. "I will not harm you."

"You have come for me?" she asked.

He shook his head. "No, I have only come to wish you well."

"But Jordh. . . ."

"Jordh gave the Allfather a choice, that he must either destroy you or else punish Brynhild for her interference," he said. "Brynhild was offered that choice in turn, and she chose the punishment for herself. She now lies asleep on that rock where you parted from her, guarded by a wall of flames. She is waiting for your son to find her, years from now. Some day they will accomplish great things. For now, she has bought with her life safety for both you and your child."

"What then?" Signy asked.

"I think that I owe you an explanation," the Wanderer replied. "You have been used, not always to your advantage, and yet you have always remained loyal."

"Brynhild has told me why it is so important."

"And do you consider that explanation enough?" he asked. "What can I say? I need your help. The Allfather

needs your help. All the Volsungs were ever needed for
was to slay one dragon. An entire race was created for that
task, and still it remains undone. But by the slaying of that
dragon, and the taking of a tiny piece of gold he protects,
whole worlds might be saved.

"Do you understand what I would say? Small tasks
might have great consequences, and yet it often seems that
small tasks are the most difficult to perform. For the want
of a small task, I have involved the Volsungs in more
trouble than I ever anticipated. I have caused you more
pain and grief than you should have ever had to endure.
You have been special to me from the beginning, and yet I
have used you shamelessly."

"I tried to believe," Signy said softly, without looking
up. She had always tried to believe, just as she was trying
to believe him now. But she had seen too much. The
promise had been broken too many times, with few reas-
surances. She had been hurt and disillusioned too many
times, and she did not want it to happen again. And she
knew that he wanted her son.

The Wanderer knew that, and knew also that he had
failed her too many times for her to trust him this once
when he was sincere. He bowed his head in sorrow and
turned away.

"I have just left Sigmund," he said. "I had thought to
bring him to see you, but he would not come. Alfheim is
home, he said, and he will not go home until you can go
with him. I see in his heart that he has been deeply hurt.
He blames himself for his failure. He has resolved to
remain a wolf forever. He does not even want to see you
in mortal form."

"That is not hard to understand. We have been taught a
very hard lesson in what we are and what we have tried to
be. As wolves we have known happiness. As men we have
known only pain and frustration and grief. We are not

meant for the world of men." She paused and looked up at the Wanderer hesitantly. "Is . . . is he well?"

He nodded. "He is as well as he can be. He misses you, but he will not come to you. He blames me, but he makes no accusations."

He paused a moment and shook his head sadly. "Sigmund was not meant to die; the sword had to be broken, to protect the both of you from Jordh's wrath. I had hoped that he would escape. If he had only been able to flee, things would have been very different. Do you know how I . . . how hard it was for the Allfather to break that sword? It was as if he had been made to slay Sigmund by his own hand."

Signy looked up at him, her eyes wide with astonishment. "Yes, I see it now."

The Wanderer turned back to her, regarding her closely. She returned his stare with mingled awe and understanding.

"I remember now, when the clouds parted and the Allfather descended upon his great horse," she said. "I remember him well. He was tall and stately, a face that was wise but terrible in wrath. He wore a patch over one eye and bore a long spear. I thought at the time that I knew him."

He nodded slowly and pulled off his hat, now a useless deception. "So now you understand all. Does that change how matters stand?"

"It changes much," Signy replied.

"I suppose that it is only just," he said as he turned to leave, leaning heavily upon his spear. "All my schemes have failed, and all my illusions have been stripped away. I would say that I am back at the very point where I started, except that I have lost so much along the way."

"Reality is truth, and truth is understanding. I understand now."

Odhinn paused and looked back at the wolfling questioningly.

"His name shall be Sigurdh," she said hesitantly. "Brynhild asked that this should be his name, so that she would know him when he came. Somehow she knew that she would be waiting for him."

"Do you trust me?"

"Never," she replied. "But I will believe with you."

"Why?"

"Because she believed," Signy said. "She stayed behind so that my son could live. If he goes back, it will be for her. Because she is waiting for him."

Odhinn nodded slowly. "She disobeyed me, and I am in her debt. Now I am in your debt as well."

He put on his hat and pulled the brim down over his face, hiding his features within its shadows. Then he took up his spear as he prepared to leave. He glanced back at the wolf-girl a final time. "I will see to it that the elves care for you and give you all the help you need."

"My lord, I am sorry. . . ," Signy said anxiously, but he held up his hand to silence her.

"No, I am sorry," he said. "I fear that I am not able to repay my debts as I should; those who do the most for me are rewarded the least. The greatest gift that I could wish for you is happiness and peace, and I can give you that only by leaving you alone. Farewell, wolfling."

He turned and walked away, and the shadows of the garden seemed to draw around him.